The
Blackwater Chronicle

THE
BLACKWATER CHRONICLE

A NARRATIVE OF AN EXPEDITION INTO

THE LAND OF CANAAN
IN RANDOLPH COUNTY, VIRGINIA

A COUNTRY FLOWING WITH WILD ANIMALS, SUCH AS PANTHERS
BEARS, WOLVES, ELK, DEER, OTTER, BADGER, &c., &c., WITH
INNUMERABLE TROUT — BY FIVE ADVENTUROUS GENTLEMEN,
WITHOUT ANY AID OF GOVERNMENT, AND SOLELY
BY THEIR OWN RESOURCES, IN THE SUMMER OF 1851

BY PHILIP PENDLETON KENNEDY

ILLUSTRATED BY DAVID HUNTER STROTHER

EDITED AND WITH A PREFACE BY
TIMOTHY SWEET

West Virginia University Press
Morgantown 2002

West Virginia University Press, Morgantown 26506
© 2002 by West Virginia University Press

First edition published 1853 by J. S. Redfield, New York.
Second Edition 2002 by West Virginia University Press
Printed in the United States of America

22 21 20 19 18 17 16 15 14   9 8 7 6 5 4 3 2

ISBN 0-937058-66-1 (alk. paper)

LIBRARY OF CONGRESS CATALOGUING-IN-PUBLICATION DATA

Kennedy, Philip Pendleton, 1808? - 1864.
    The Blackwater chronicle : a narrative of an expedition into
    the land of Canaan, in Randolph county, Virginia, a country
    flowing with wild animals, such as panthers, bears, wolves,
    elk, deer, otter, badger, &c., &c., with innumerable trout—
    by five adventurous gentlemen, without any aid of govern-
    ment, and solely by their own resources, in the summer of
    1851/ by "the Clerke of Oxenforde" [i.e. Philip Pendleton
    Kennedy]; with ill. from life by [David Hunter] Strother;
    edited by Timothy Sweet.
           p. cm. — (West Virginia and Appalachia ; 2)
1. Canaan Valley (W. Va.) — Description and travel. 2. Blackwater River (W. Va.) — Description and travel. I. Title. II. Kennedy,
Philip Pendleton, 1808?-1864. III. Sweet, Timothy. IV. Series.
IN PROCESS

Library of Congress Control Number: 2002108430

Design by Alcorn Publication Design
Illustrations are derived from a copy of the first edition (1853)
    in the West Virginia Collection, West Virginia University
    Libraries

CONTENTS

PREFACE

BY TIMOTHY SWEET

In late May of 1851, a party of sportsmen from the Shenandoah valley of Virginia set out on a 'pleasure expedition' to the North Branch of the Potomac River. They intended to spend their days fishing for trout and their evenings enjoying 'an easy, lounging time of it about the porches' of Edward Towers's inn at Winston.[1] And so they did, until one evening when someone happened to mention ' "THE CANAAN," or wilderness-country, over on the head-waters of the Cheat.' Intrigued by reports that 'this land of Canaan was as perfect a wilderness as our continent contained,' the party determined to explore the area. Employing two local hunters as guides, they started south from the headwaters of the Potomac, several miles above Towers's inn. After two days of 'the roughest and hardest sort of walking and climbing,' they found the North Fork of the Blackwater River and followed it down to the 'grand, picturesque' series of falls and pools where it cascades into Blackwater Canyon.[2] Neither of the guides had been this far downstream before. The innkeeper had promised the party that 'if you can only reach the falls of the Blackwater, you can take more trout in an hour than you ever took before in all your lives.' They were not disappointed.

Philip Pendleton Kennedy's account of this adventure makes for enjoyable reading today. More than this, however, the book provides both an interesting glimpse into antebellum American literary culture and an important record of the Canaan wilderness before it was despoiled by economic exploitation. These qualities make *The Blackwater Chronicle* a work of lasting value.

KENNEDY'S LIFE AND WRITINGS

Philip Pendleton Kennedy—'Pent,' as he was called by family and friends throughout his life—was the youngest of four brothers.[3] Born in Baltimore in 1808, he spent much of his childhood in western Virginia. His mother, Nancy Clay Pendleton, descended from an eminent family that could trace its Virginia lineage back to the seventeenth century. Nancy married John Kennedy of Baltimore, who had a successful business supplying copper sheeting to shipbuilders. Nancy and the children spent summers among her family in Jefferson and Berkeley counties, returning to Baltimore in winter. Pent was born just as hard times hit the shipping trade following the Embargo of 1807. His father was forced to declare bankruptcy in 1809, and thereafter the family's main source of income was Clayton, an estate near Charles Town in the Shenandoah valley that Nancy inherited from her father. In about 1820, the family moved to Clayton, leaving eldest son John in Baltimore to practice law.

No record remains of Pent's childhood, and relatively little from his adult life. One hint does survive however in a memoir of his cousin, the poet Philip Pendleton Cooke, which Pent wrote at age forty-three. There he reflects 'on the passion that the life of childhood experiences in many and most cases, perhaps in all—the sad and sometimes tragic terrors that children endure.—The greifs [sic] even to death of children. . . . If it is thus in childhood, what may not be predicated of the manhood of a human being! Let us not then forget, what trials and strifes of passion men endure with silence, . . . —remorse, revenge, hatred, thwarted ambition, the pangs of despised love, keen-felt ingratitude, burning shame.'[4] Although we can do no more than speculate, we cannot help but bear this commentary in mind as we review Pent's life and literary career.

We do know this much: an 1871 biography of his brother John characterized Pent as 'an erratic genius' who became 'the victim of unfortunate habits'—which is to say that he gambled and drank heavily.[5] Pent was a familiar sight at horse races in the lower Shenandoah valley. He ran up debts, which John sometimes helped him repay. He loved to fish and hunt, although he took less interest in hunting after he shot himself in the right leg. This accident, he reports in *The Blackwater Chronicle*, left his leg 'shortened and stiffened at the knee.' He studied law for a time, at age twenty, but if he envisioned any career for himself, it was that of professional writer. Or it might be as accurate to say that others, especially John, envisioned such a career for him.

While Pent no doubt appreciated John's encouragement, he probably also felt overshadowed by his brother's successful career as author, lawyer, and statesman. Best remembered today for his humorous portrayal of plantation life in *Swallow Barn* (1832), John also published two other novels, *Horse-Shoe Robinson* (1835) and *Rob of the Bowl* (1838), a political satire, *Quodlibet* (1840), and miscellaneous works. His political career culminated in his appointment as Secretary of the Navy under Millard Fillmore in 1852, while his prominence in southern letters— second at the time only to that of William Gilmore Simms—was confirmed by the successful republication of his novels in 1850, 1852, and 1854. During this period, he particularly encouraged Pent to embark on a literary career.

In 1850, Rufus Griswold, one of the leading literary figures of the day, took over as editor of the *International Monthly Magazine*. Looking for material, Griswold asked John to contribute a 'sketch' of the 'life and writing' of the above mentioned Philip Pendleton Cooke, who had recently died. Since cousin Cooke was a hunting and fishing companion of Pent's, John thought Pent might do well by his memory. In May, he urged Pent to write the memoir 'and send it to me as soon as you can. . . . Griswold is waiting for it.'[6] Pent was slow in sending the manuscript, and by September John viewed the matter with greater urgency. It is likely that Pent was in financial difficulty, for John advised, 'by all means and every sacrifice avoid debt' and 'employ yourself in something that will pay your expenses: that is, practice law in Martinsburg, or write as well as you can.' By writing for the magazines, 'a good article every fortnight,' he might 'make some six or seven hundred dollars every year.'[7] Pent managed to produce a draft by the following March and sent it to John to critique, which he did at great length.[8] By then, Griswold had lost interest. Another likely prospect for publication was William Gilmore Simms's *Southern Quarterly Review*, which was dedicated to promoting southern writers. Pent evidently promised Simms the manuscript, but in February of 1852, Simms wrote to John that he had 'waited for it in vain.'[9] In any case, it is unlikely that the piece would have been published without extensive revision. John judged the style 'too distressingly *intense*,' wondering what had happened to Pent's former 'fine, clear, transparent style,' which was now 'bedevilled and bemystified . . . with such cracking of heart-strings, and subjectivity of emotion.'[10] While John's assessment is apt, the memoir does retain some of that clear style in one episode, a 'ludicrous adventure' in which young Phil Cooke comes to court his sweetheart one night only to get treed by 'an old fierce 'Possum and 'Coon dog.'[11] The gift for comic incident shown here would serve Pent well as he composed *The Blackwater Chronicle*.

Pent had been working on another article for the magazines as well, a review essay on Hugh Garland's *Life of John Randolph of Roanoke*. Again, John critiqued the draft extensively and used his literary connections to try to get it published. Pent thought immediately of Simms, but John concluded that the article 'will not do for the Southern [Quarterly] Review.' Unlike the memoir of Cooke, this piece had to deal with political topics; we can surmise that it did not support Simms's extreme 'Southron' views. The *American Whig Review* was a more appropriate venue. John had contacted the editor, James Whelply, 'asking him what he would pay for it,' but had received no response 'although it is weeks since I wrote.'[12] He then sent the manuscript to his good friend Robert C. Winthrop of Boston, who knew the editors of both the *Christian Examiner* and the *North American Review*, stating that 'I should like whoever gets it to pay [Pent] for it.' He had, he confided to Winthrop, 'encouraged' Pent 'to believe' that he could get 'a literary recognition of merit' and this would be a first step.[13] Winthrop was not encouraging. He replied that Francis Bowen of the *Examiner* often 'rejects what other men think good,' while even acceptance by the *North American* did not necessarily augur a promising career. Winthrop himself had found that remuneration 'for literary effort in these parts is pretty small,' punning that the *North American* 'pays a doleur [*sic*] a page.'[14] Although neither the Cooke nor the Garland project bore fruit, John encouraged Pent to 'persevere in your purpose of writing for the periodicals,' especially since his finances continued to be problematic.[15]

Meanwhile, Pent turned to a new genre. In late May of 1851, he and some friends embarked on the trip that resulted in *The Blackwater Chronicle*. These friends, identified only by comic pseudonyms in the book, included artist David Hunter Strother ('Signor Andante Strozzi').[16] Perhaps Pent conceived the idea of writing an amusing travel narrative as they planned the trip. Strother may have encouraged the idea, for he had traveled avidly in America and Europe in search of material, sometimes keeping journals as well as making sketches.[17] Of course he would bring pencil and paper on this trip as well. At the outset, however, neither could have predicted the book's final shape, for the Blackwater adventure itself was conceived on the spur of the moment, in desultory conversation one evening at Towers's inn.

In April of 1852, Pent and Strother traveled to New York where they 'made some arrangements' with J. S. Redfield to publish the book.[18] Redfield was a well established firm with a varied list. It held copyright to Poe's works and had published some of Simms's novels, Alice Cary's highly popular

Clovernook sketches, an edition of Shakespeare, as well as works of history, biography, travel, natural history, and medicine. Strother's involvement may have helped to sell Redfield on the *Blackwater* project, since he had already gained some recognition as an illustrator of books such as the Harper and Brothers *Illuminated Bible*, the second edition of *Swallow Barn*, and Simms's *Life of Captain John Smith*.[19] We do not know the nature of the publishing contract. Standard arrangements at the time included author-risk (in which the author assumed manufacturing costs, including commission for illustrations), half-profit (in which the publisher assumed costs and split the net returns with the author), or straight royalty (usually 10 percent of the retail price).[20] It seems likely that Pent's contract was author-risk, for in a letter of July 2, 1852, John told him, 'I regret it is not in my power to help you with the money arrangement to which you refer, as I am now under engagements which will absorb all in funds I can command next year.' John also mentions having paid Pent's 'previous draft . . . to the amount of $189.7[0],' noting that his debts still amounted to 'about $900.'[21] Assuming that Pent could have delivered the fair copy manuscript on or soon after the April 1852 meeting with Redfield, there was an unusual delay in bringing out the book. Financial arrangements may have played a part in this delay.

The Blackwater Chronicle was published in November of 1853. Pent had been 'daily awaiting' the event since September, when it was advertised in *Putnam's* as forthcoming.[22] The book made some mark in the literary world, garnering reviews in the *Southern Literary Messenger* and the *Southern Quarterly Review* and a brief notice in *Harper's Monthly*. Anthology editor William Burton included an excerpt in his 1858 *Cyclopaedia of Wit and Humor*. The book also gained some international recognition, as editions were soon published in London and Leipzig.[23]

An unknown quantity such as *The Blackwater Chronicle* could easily get lost in the literary world unless someone looked out for it. Strother's name on the title page as illustrator probably helped in this regard, at least with *Harper's Monthly*.[24] In December 1853, *Harper's* published Strother's illustrated story of a second Blackwater expedition.[25] The next month, drawing the connection to Strother's 'humorous account,' *Harper's* predicted that *Blackwater* 'has all the elements of a wide popularity.'[26] Despite the book's pseudonymous publication, reviewers evidently knew the author's identity. The *Southern Literary Messenger* did not name the author but said that his 'literary tastes, shining wit, and exuberant fancy, ought long ago to have been exemplified in a book.' While the 'humorous descriptions' provided 'an afternoon's enjoyment,' the reviewer felt that *Blackwater* did not finally 'come up to our notion of what its gifted author could accomplish; if he chose.'[27]

William Gilmore Simms, who after all had met Pent and knew his brother well, was more generous, praising the author's 'play with his subject as a zephyr with its wing.' The writing 'flies, with most pleasant and capricious fancy, over the fields of the new Canaan which was thus penetrated and laid open to souls that thirst for cool waters and a delicious empire.' Yet Simms too characterized the author as 'the possessor of talents which he himself has too little valued to use. But we will not point him out to the inquisitive. Let him make himself better known by his deeds.'[28]

Thus *Blackwater*'s reception among the southern critics must have felt uncannily familiar to Pent, for this had long been his brother's view of him: that he had great potential but did not quite realize his promise. John himself, however, expressed no such reservations in this instance. He recommended the book to Winthrop and noted in his journal that he was 'delighted with it. It is so joyous and fresh with the finest artistic tints of the landscape paper.' He thought also that the rigors of the 'expedition' were 'so graphically described that I suspect the reader of this book has the best part of the enterprise.' As to Pent's own reflection on his work, we have only John's remark that Pent 'has been very happy in this his first essay.'[29]

Unfortunately this first 'essay' in print was also his last. Pent did continue to write, but nothing more was published.[30] The death of his mother in 1853 left him a small inheritance, including a house in Martinsburg and one servant, so he did not need to publish in order to survive. He remained in Martinsburg during the war and was imprisoned by Confederate forces during the spring of 1862. The captivity broke his health, long weakened by drink in any case. Fleeing another Confederate attack on the Shenandoah valley in 1864, he went to his brother Anthony's home in Maryland, where he died of pneumonia on August 1. It remained to his long time friend Strother to redress the balance regarding Pent's character: 'Philosophers would say here was a life thrown away. I don't see it. He enjoyed and lived his life on an average as much as others. He charmed and annoyed his circle of friends as others do. He made some mark socially while he lived. He might have done better, and who might not?'[31]

THE BLACKWATER CHRONICLE IN LITERARY CONTEXT

By Kennedy's time, the wilderness adventure was a venerable and varied American genre. We can trace its lineage from seventeenth-century exploration and settlement narratives by the likes of Captain John Smith and Thomas Morton through William Byrd's *History of the Dividing Line* and *Secret History of the Line* (1729) to Washington Irving's *A Tour on the Prairies* (1834), Francis Parkman's *The Oregon Trail* (1849), or Henry David Thoreau's *The Maine Woods* (1865). Kennedy's style owes more to eighteenth-century wit than to the journalistic approach of Irving or Parkman. He shares with Byrd a comfortable manner of never taking himself or his adventures too seriously, while his device of giving the company humorous names particularly recalls the *Secret History*.[32] Kennedy does not indulge in the ribaldry of the *Secret History* but achieves comic effects through puns, raillery, mock-heroic conceits, and other verbal play. There were influences beyond the genre as well, of course. Since *Tristram Shandy* and *A Sentimental Journey* were both great favorites of Kennedy's brother John, for example, some readers hear echoes of Laurence Sterne.[33] Regardless of influences, few writers capture so well as Kennedy the genial banter of male camaraderie.

This light and humorous vein sets *The Blackwater Chronicle* apart from the contemporarily popular transcendentalist mode. The habit of moralizing the landscape, of reading nature as God's book, was well established in American travel writing by the 1830s.[34] Such an approach could yield great insight at the hands of a master such as Thoreau but often proved barren. A typical example is *The Adirondack* by best-selling author Joel Tyler Headley, a book that bears particular comparison to *Blackwater* because it too recounts a trout-fishing expedition into wilderness country. Headley writes, for example, that 'a single tree standing alone, and waving its green crown in the summer wind, is to me fuller of meaning and instruction than the crowded mart or gorgeously built town,' but he is incapable of suggesting what such meaning might be.[35] Kennedy does give us one transcendental moment in which an aesthetic response to nature evokes 'that perfect bliss of the soul . . . which has no taint of our mortal lot in it.' Yet he is more interested in the effects of the wilderness setting on the expedition's social dynamic: 'we feel an unbounded liberty; . . . there is such entire freedom of remark among us, one to another, . . . such careless luxuriance of attitude.' While some interaction bespeaks a freedom 'too great' to be set down in writing 'even in this outspoken age,' Kennedy does present numerous milder instances. For example, when the 'melancholy soughing' of the wind through the trees at night 'awakened our superstition, and no diversion of thought could dispossess our souls of its influence,' Master Philip mocks the cowards by singing a ghostly ballad, complete with wailing banshee, 'in a low, wild voice, all in harmony with the soughing sound of the firs'—to which Adolphus responds, 'Hush your horrible croaking! . . . Isn't it all miserable enough already, but you must be keeping us from going to sleep with ballads about dying men, and such unearthly things?' They threaten to throw this latter-day Ossian into the river, but the banter continues until Signor Andante, 'tun[ing] his voice' to the 'sobbing and sighing wind,' warms up with 'The Twa Corbies' and then leads the company in selections from the opera 'Robert the Devil,' to the 'utter amazement' of the hunters Powell and Conway.[36]

Kennedy plays with other conventions of the genre as well. In the antebellum era, the shadow of Europe fell heavily on the American landscape. Headley, for example, used the Alps as a constant point of reference for mountain scenery in *The Adirondack.* Irving found the grandeur of a Gothic cathedral in the Arkansas forests, while Parkman responded to his first view of Pike's Peak by quoting a stanza from Byron's *Childe Harold.* James Fenimore Cooper's essay 'American and European Scenery Compared' assembled the commonplaces on this topic at mid-century.[37] Kennedy too at one point describes the forest canopy by campfire light as 'the lighted tracery of some vast Gothic minster of the wild.' Yet since little remained to be said in this vein, he devotes more time to a humorous treatment. As Master Philip launches a grand oration accusing the English of unjustly disparaging the American landscape, the company interject in mock encouragement: 'Don't go in any deeper . . . or the subject will swim you'; 'It's a great spouting! A whale's!'; 'What a senator he would make!'; and so on. Signor Andante points out that for all this, Philip hasn't really addressed the topic of comparison. He could do so himself, he says, 'but we can't stay here all day.'[38] For the most part, Kennedy's approach to landscape description ignores European comparisons to concentrate on the scene before him. Occasionally he splashes the descriptions with a poetic quotation or an amusing image to make us look again at the mental picture he has led us to paint; in one such image, the Blackwater 'leaps over the falls like a river of calf's-foot jelly with a spray of whipped syllabub on top of it.'

A distinctive feature of Kennedy's style is an abundant and wide-ranging use of quotation and allusion. In the above-mentioned speech, for example, Philip cites the Bible and Lord Nelson, the *Iliad* and Francis Drake, and so on without pause. This allusive style begins on the title page, where the author is identified as 'The Clerke of Oxenforde,' evoking Chaucer's account of a rather different sort of pilgrimage in the *Canterbury Tales*. Early on, Kennedy 'impresse[s]' on the reader 'a due sense of the dignity of our undertaking' by developing an extended mock-heroic conceit, humorously comparing the upcoming expedition to the exploits of Caesar in Gaul, and his chronicle of the expedition to histories by Thucydides, Livy, Voltaire, and Macaulay (although not to Caesar's own writing of course, which lacks a certain literary polish). A great student of songs and ballads, he quotes several as sung by the party, thereby enhancing his depiction of their camaraderie. In sum, Kennedy draws effortlessly on classical and modern literature alike, with the exception of the novel. *Don Quixote* is appropriately mentioned, but the modern novel (interestingly, his brother's primary genre) largely escapes Kennedy's notice. If at one point he populates the landscape with figures from classical mythology (Diana, Endymion, Pan), he reflects self-consciously on the literary game he plays: 'I am fully aware that in here giving expression to these fancies, I run some little risk of stamping this historic narrative with the character of fiction.'

Kennedy's penchant for quotation and allusion may feel artificial today. Even so, it provides significant insight into antebellum literary culture, reminding us that literature was as great a presence in Kennedy's daily life as photographs, television, or film are in ours—and that writers, like photographers and filmmakers, often pay homage (deliberate or not) to their forebears. Kennedy's style can thus alert us to the ways in which our experience of nature is always framed by a history of words and images. As we enjoy his lively and erudite account of the Blackwater adventure, we can reflect on the reservoir of culture that we bring to nature.

THE BLACKWATER CHRONICLE AND ENVIRONMENTAL HISTORY

In 1851, the Blackwater region remained wild, much as the Fairfax Boundary Line surveying party had found it a century earlier. This wilderness would soon be despoiled by economic exploitation. *The Blackwater Chronicle*, together with other early accounts by Thomas Lewis (1746), David Hunter Strother (1853 and 1873), and Rebecca Harding Davis (1880), thus provides an important record of the region's environmental history.[39]

Kennedy's Blackwater expedition started from the source of the North Branch of the Potomac. According to Thomas Lewis's journal of the Fairfax survey, the Potomac headwaters region was 'Exceeding well timberd' with 'very Large Spruce pines' and 'great multituds' of oak, hickory, beech, sugar maple, and black cherry, some 'three or four foot' in diameter and rising 'thirty or forty foot without a Branch.'[40] A hundred years later, Kennedy too remarks on 'the great size of the trees' and diversity of species here: 'a most noble forest of sugar-trees, the beech, maple, wild-cherry, balsam-firs, and hemlocks.' In the 'slight clearings' of this forest grew 'wild timothy' grass.[41]

As the party journeyed from the Potomac toward the North Fork of the Blackwater, they saw the mixed forest give way to great stands of hemlock and balsam fir, the latter at the southernmost limit of its natural range.[42] When the trees reached maturity and died, their trunks fell to the forest floor. Kennedy thus remarks a characteristic feature of these old-growth woods: the Blackwater party would often 'come up against a barrier of fallen trees—some of them six feet high as they lay along the ground, and coated with moss a half a foot thick—some so decomposed that they recreated themselves in the young hemlocks and firs that grew up out of them.' Rebecca Harding Davis would also remark this ongoing cycle of decay and regeneration: 'Huge trees, fallen a century before, lay in gigantic round furrows on the ground; furrows of deep moss, of fretted and fluted lichen, gray and golden, bronze and purple, and of trailing myriads of pink oxalis. Plumy fern nodded from the sides, and a thicket of young hemlocks pushed ambitiously up from the top of the ridge; but when Jerry put his foot on it, the whole furrow crumbled like a puff-ball into a cloud of dust. It was a dead body, which, undisturbed in the slow passage of unaccounted years, had made all this false show of life.'[43] Comparing the writers' responses to the deceptive insolidity of the decayed trunks, we can observe that where Davis moralizes on a 'false show of life,' Kennedy and Strother both use such an image humorously to reveal the travelers' lack of woodcraft: often someone tries to clamber along a downed trunk only to fall through, finding himself 'embedded to the armpits, in what he had supposed to be solid wood,' much to the amusement of his companions.[44]

In the moist soils of the bottoms grew dense thickets of the 'big laurel' (*Rhododendron maximum*), some extending 'as far as the eye could reach, like a green lake, with either shore walled by the massive forest.'[45] Kennedy noticed 'the glory of its flower, now just swelling into bloom' in early June. The Fairfax survey party, traversing the region in October, did not see the flowers, but they might not have remarked them in any case. They had such trouble getting through the thickets that, as Lewis wrote, 'nor Ever was a Criminal more glad By having made his Escape out of prison as we were to Get Rid of those Accursed Lorals.'[46] Davis too would see something ominous in these thickets, harborage for bears, panthers, and wolves; she was especially disturbed by the 'red and black spiders' that 'swung themselves incessantly across [the travelers'] faces.'[47] The Blackwater party found the laurel inconvenient to be sure, but also useful. At one point early on, knowing that the terrain would soon become too rugged for horses, they located a grassy dale in the Potomac glades 'girt round upon its edges by a broad belt of the *Rhododendron*'; here they corralled the horses for several days until they could return for them, 'barricad[ing] the entrance by piling up some young trees and brushwood (which was equivalent to putting up the bars in a fenced field).'

The streams of the Blackwater drainage, tinted a characteristic deep amber by tannins from decaying hemlock needles, held native brook trout in great abundance, many as large as 'thirteen inches long' and 'three inches deep behind the shoulders.' Kennedy's description of two color variants is particularly interesting. He reports that half the fish taken from the North Fork were 'black trout, with deep red spots,' the typical coloration of the brook trout. Equally prevalent however were 'salmon-colored' trout 'with lighter red spots.' Both of these must have been brook trout (*Salvelinus fontinalis*), for browns and rainbows had not yet been introduced to any eastern American waters, but no 'salmon-colored' variant is known today. Thus it is possible that Kennedy recorded here the existence of a unique local trout population which was extirpated as a result of subsequent environmental degradation.[48]

Kennedy knew that economic development would alter this wilderness environment: since 'the railroad will bring all this region within a day's travel of the seaboard, . . . it is not irrational to suppose that it will be cleared out and settled with rapidity.' He saw two possible paths for development. In one, 'the coal' would be 'dug out of the earth, and the ores, the gypsum, the salt, and the lumber, turned into wealth.' Adolphus and Botecote, however, imagine an agrarian alternative to this extractive economy. They would buy vast acreages, hire laborers to 'belt' some of the woods, and graze cattle on the timothy grass that would spring up beneath the girdled trees. Such an enterprise would support a life of aristocratic leisure compatible to some extent with preservationist values, for they would 'have the Canaan as a park,' a habitat for 'bears and panthers—elk at the least.' They imagine 'their houses . . . filled, during the summer months, with gentlemen and ladies, who hunted and rode, fished, eat the trout, . . . grew fat and defied the world below, in the pastimes of the wilderness.' Yet while cattle production had flourished in the South Branch, Greenbrier, and Shenandoah valleys since the 1780s, it would never play a significant economic role in the Blackwater region. Strother's 1873 description of a typical small farmstead thus deflates the pastoral fantasy: 'Skeleton forests, leafless, lifeless, weather-beaten, and fire-blasted; heaps of withered branches; split rail fences, warped and rotten; barns and out-buildings bare-ribbed, and grizzled with premature decay; wretched frames of domestic animals covered with moth-eaten hides, and strolling about like lifeless automatons; a dwelling dingy, contorted, and dilapidated, in the midst of a space from whence every green thing and graceful form has been banished.'[49]

The region's resources were brought to market not through agrarian settlement but through timber and coal extraction. The completion of the Baltimore and Ohio line from Cumberland to Wheeling in 1852, just a year after Kennedy's expedition, marked the beginning of commercial timbering. Logs were floated down the Cheat in spring flood to the railhead at Rowlesburg. Operations remained small and localized, however, confined mainly to the lower Cheat, until the West Virginia Central and Pittsburgh railroad opened the entire headwaters region to exploitation. The railroad reached Thomas in 1884 and Elkins in 1889 and spurs were soon built throughout the region. On the main stem of the Blackwater at Davis, two lumber mills, a pulp mill, and a tannery (which used hemlock bark) were in operation by 1895, processing trees into commodities and dumping their wastes into the river. The Blackwater Canyon proved especially difficult for logging operations until steam-powered skidders were brought in to haul

logs off the steep slopes. Lack of forest cover result-
ing from clear-cutting caused soil erosion and stream
siltation. Ironically though, it did not reduce the risk
of fire, since the litter of the forest floor dried to a
combustible peat on exposure to the sun. In 1914, a
fire in the logged-off Blackwater Canyon burned for
six months. The coal industry also wrought great
environmental changes, creating a severe acid mine
drainage problem. On the North Fork, a mine was
opened just below Thomas in 1886, and others followed. The coal proved suitable for coking and soon,
as a local historian put it, 'the glow of a thousand
coke ovens' in the night sky resembled 'the aurora
borealis.'[50] Today the ruins of these ovens line the
banks of the North Fork, a visible reminder of the
river's industrial history.

By 1920, the entire region had been deforested
and much of it mined, its streams ruined.[51] Today,
in some areas, mixed deciduous species have re-
placed the ancient stands of hemlock, fir, and
spruce.[52] Other areas remain deforested. As a result, ambient temperatures throughout the region
are higher than they were in Kennedy's time. Water
temperatures too are higher and more variable, di-
minishing the streams' capacities to support trout
and other aquatic life. The North Fork of the Blackwater in particular suffers from acid mine drainage.
Throughout the North Fork watershed, acidified
waters carrying high iron loads pour from old mine
portals and groundwater seeps, severely compromis-

ing stream quality. Restoration efforts have begun with the construction of a wetland treatment system near Douglas; however, much more is needed. On the main stem of the Blackwater above the North Fork, acidification is being successfully treated by a crushed limestone system. While the main stem has recovered enough to be regularly stocked with fish (browns and rainbows in addition to the native brook trout), it is currently affected by pollution from other industries. As of this writing, a legal battle rages over the allowable level of pollutants discharged into the main stem. Acid rain poses an additional threat to forest and stream ecology in the Blackwater region and elsewhere. As restoration efforts are mounted and debates over environmental use continue, *The Blackwater Chronicle* reminds us of the region's former, wilderness state.

THE BLACKWATER CHRONICLE IN RETROSPECT

In its day, *The Blackwater Chronicle* was an amusing tale of wilderness adventure. A century and a half after its first publication, it has become a significant document of Appalachian environmental history and an interesting example of antebellum literary culture. Yet for all that, it is still an enjoyable story, a good read.

Part of the book's charm lies in the engravings made from David Hunter Strother's sketches, which add another dimension to Kennedy's verbal descriptions. Two of the engravings focus exclusively on natural objects: the frontispiece and half-title page give picturesque views of a deer and a cascading stream—as at times Kennedy sketches similar scenes in prose. Most of the illustrations, however, show social action in nature, giving visual emphasis to Kennedy's account of the camaraderie of the adventure.[53] The tone is set in Chapter III as the party meet an itinerant minstrel on the road from Winchester; in Strother's sketch, the men dance while the minstrel cranks an organ. In Chapter X, we see Peter Botecote tossing a mess of trout in a frying pan for the hungry Master Philip. Even the view of towering hemlocks in Chapter IX shows the party relaxing of an evening in their 'lodge in the wilderness.' The book ends on an outdoor still-life—kettle hanging over the fire, rifle and string of trout nearby—which recalls the pleasures of the foregoing adventure. We share the nostalgia evoked by this sketch as we reach *The Blackwater Chronicle*'s final page, a nostalgia complicated by the literary and environmental histories of the intervening years.

A Note on the Text and Illustrations

The text of the present edition has been set in Bookman Old Style to approximate the font of the first edition. Obvious typographical errors have been silently corrected; spelling irregularities, often meant to indicate dialect, have been retained to preserve

Kennedy's style. The illustrations have been digitally reproduced from a copy of the first edition held by the West Virginia and Regional History Collection, West Virginia University.[54] The illustrations have been placed in the text so as to replicate the general appearance of *The Blackwater Chronicle* as it was first offered to the reading public in 1853.

Notes

1. Towers's inn, located near what is now Gormania, West Virginia, was a popular 'resort for sportsmen before the [Civil] war'; see Rebecca Harding Davis, 'By-Paths in the Mountains—I,' *Harper's New Monthly Magazine* 61 (July 1880): 173.

2. Kennedy refers to the North Fork of the Blackwater as 'the Blackwater' and to the main stem of the Blackwater as 'the Cheat.' The party did not reach the falls that today are the main attraction of Blackwater Falls State Park, about three miles above the North Fork's confluence with the main stem, nor did they see the Canaan Valley some five miles to the east. The first literary record of the great falls of the Blackwater is David Hunter Strother, 'The Mountains—VII,' *Harper's New Monthly Magazine* 47 (Nov. 1873): 828-29.

3. The only biography is Cecil D. Eby, Jr., 'Philip Pendleton Kennedy: Author of *The Blackwater Chronicle*,' *West Virginia History* 22 (Oct. 1960): 5-13. Information for the following sketch is taken from Eby and from Charles H. Bohner, *John Pendleton Kennedy: Gentleman from Baltimore* (Baltimore: Johns Hopkins University Press, 1961).

4. Philip Pendleton Kennedy, memoir of Philip Pendleton Cooke. Typescript (original manuscript lost), West Virginia and Regional History Collection, West Virginia University,

ms. no. 1225, 22.

5. Henry T. Tuckerman, *The Life of John Pendleton Kennedy* (New York: G. P. Putnam, 1871), 26.

6. John Pendleton Kennedy, letter to Philip Pendleton Kennedy (hereafter JPK and PPK), May ? (illegible), 1850. All letters and journal entries are cited from the microfilm edition of the John Pendleton Kennedy papers, which are held by the Peabody Institute. For information on the papers, see John B. Boles, *A Guide to the Microfilm Edition of the John Pendleton Kennedy Papers* (Baltimore: Enoch Pratt Free Library and Maryland Historical Society, 1972).

7. JPK, letter to PPK, Sept. 28, 1850.

8. JPK, journal, Mar. 17, 1851.

9. Simms, letter to JPK, Feb. 17, 1852.

10. JPK, letter to PPK, Apr. 10, 1851, underlining in original.

11. Kennedy, memoir of Cooke, 12.

12. JPK, letter to PPK, Apr. 10, 1851. Simms soon published a scathing review of the book; *Southern Quarterly Review* 4 (July 1851): 41-61. On John's Whig politics and his break with Simms, see Bohner, 226-27.

13. JPK, letter to Winthrop, Apr. 21, 1851.

14. Winthrop, letter to JPK, Apr. 23, 1851.

15. JPK, letter to PPK, July 2, 1852.

16. The others were Dr. E. Boyd Pendleton ('Dr. Adolphus Blandy' or 'Galen'), Frank Peters ('Botecote' or 'Butcut'), Edmund J. Lee ('Guy Philips, Master of the priory of St. Philips'), and Pent himself ('Triptolemus Todd' or 'Murad the Unlucky'). Eby (10) makes these identifications from JPK, journal, June 20, 1851.

17. On Strother's travels, see John Cuthbert, *David Hunter Strother: 'One of the Best Draughtsman the Country Possesses'* (Morgantown: West Virginia University Press, 1997), 13-20. Cuthbert reproduces two sketches from the 1851 Blackwater expedition (85, 87). The latter of these was used for the half-title page of *The Blackwater Chronicle*.

18. JPK, journal, May 1, 1852.

19. Cuthbert, 26.
20. On such arrangements, see William Charvat, *Literary Publishing in America, 1790-1850* (1953; rpt. Amherst: University of Massachusetts Press, 1993), 38-60; Susan Coultrap-McQuin, *Doing Literary Business: American Women Writers in the Nineteenth Century* (Chapel Hill: University of North Carolina Press, 1990), 40, 124, 207.
21. JPK, letter to PPK, July 2, 1852.
22. JPK, letter to Adele Granger, Sept. 29, 1853.
23. *Narrative of an Expedition of Five Americans into a Country of Wild Animals* (London: James Blackwood, 1854), illustrated by English artist and playwright Watts Phillips; *Blackwater; oder, eine Entdreckungsreise in das Land Canaan*, trans. W. E. Drugulin (Leipzig, 1855), not illustrated. See Eby, 5. Since then the book has been reprinted once: *The Blackwater Chronicle* (Parsons, W. Va.: West Virginia Department of Natural Resources-McClain Printing Co., 1978).
24. Because *Blackwater* was published pseudonymously while Strother is named as illustrator, the text was erroneously attributed to Strother in Daniel Lucas's 1909 *A Library of Southern Literature*; see Eby, 5. It has also been attributed to John Pendleton Kennedy, an error that persists in some library catalogs.
25. 'The Virginia Canaan,' *Harper's New Monthly Magazine* 8 (Dec. 1853): 18-36. This expedition of June 1852 also included Pent. They went as far as Pendleton Creek, which Strother calls the 'Black Fork of Cheat.'
26. *Harper's New Monthly Magazine* 8 (Jan. 1854): 287.
27. *Southern Literary Messenger* 29 (Dec. 1853): 779.
28. *Southern Quarterly Review* 9 (Jan. 1854): 268-69.
29. JPK, letter to Winthrop, Dec. 4, 1853; JPK, journal, Nov. 13, 1853.
30. On his death in 1864 Pent left a large collection of manuscripts and papers, which John burned, except for the memoir of Cooke. See Bohner, 190.
31. Qtd. in Eby, 13.

32. It is quite possible that Kennedy knew, or knew of Byrd's *History*, since an edition was published by fellow Virginian Edmund Ruffin in 1841. The *Secret History* is another matter. A manuscript had been on deposit at the American Philosophical Society since 1818. John Pendleton Kennedy was elected a member of the Society in 1852 and may have known of this manuscript. At least two other fragments of the *Secret History* existed in manuscript copy as well; their provenances are complicated. See *The Prose Works of William Byrd of Westover*, ed. Louis B. Wright (Cambridge: Belknap-Harvard University Press, 1966), 421-22.

33. Eby, 10. On John's fondness for Sterne, see Bohner, 13.

34. See for example Kenneth John Myers, 'On the Cultural Construction of the Landscape: Contact to 1830,' in David C. Miller, ed., *American Iconology: New Approaches to Nineteenth-Century Art and Literature* (New Haven: Yale University Press, 1993), 58-79.

35. Joel Tyler Headley, *The Adirondack; or, Life in the Woods* (New York: Baker and Scribner, 1849), 168.

36. This episode exemplifies Kennedy's allusive style, discussed below. The ballad 'Rossmore' derives from the legend surrounding the mysterious death of Lord Rossmore in 1801, as reported for example in Sir Jonah Barrington's *Personal Sketches* (1827); I have not been able to identify a source for the ballad itself. 'The Twa Corbies' is from Sir Walter Scott's *Minstrelsy of the Scottish Border* (1802-03). *Robert le Diable*, an opera by Giacomo Meyerbeer, was first performed in Paris in 1831 and in New York in 1834.

37. Cooper, 'American and European Scenery Compared,' in *The Home Book of the Picturesque: Or, American Scenery, Art, and Literature* (New York: G. P. Putnam, 1852), 51-69.

38. This is the passage that William Burton chose to reprint in his *Cyclopaedia of Wit and Humor* (New York: D. Appleton, 1858), 339-41.

39. *The Fairfax Line: Thomas Lewis's Journal of 1746* (New Market, Va.: Henkel Press, 1925); David Hunter Strother,

'The Virginia Canaan,' *Harper's New Monthly Magazine* 8 (Dec. 1853): 18-36, reprinted in *Virginia Illustrated* (New York: Harper and Brothers, 1857), 13-51; Strother, 'The Mountains—VII,' *Harper's New Monthly Magazine* 46 (Apr. 1873): 669-80; Strother, 'The Mountains—VIII,' *Harper's New Monthly Magazine* 47 (Nov. 1873): 821-32; Rebecca Harding Davis, 'By-Paths in the Mountains—I,' *Harper's New Monthly Magazine* 61 (July 1880): 167-85.

40. *Fairfax Line*, 39. 'Spruce pine' is a common name for hemlock; see P. D. Strausbaugh and Earl L. Core, *Flora of West Virginia*, 2nd ed. (Morgantown, W. Va.: Seneca Books, n.d.), 46. It is interesting to note that none of the early accounts mentions the yellow or tulip poplar, now so frequent in these woods.

41. Timothy was not native to the region. Imported from England in the 1630s, it was introduced from New England to Maryland in the 1720s. See William Cronon, *Changes in the Land: Indians, Colonists, and the Ecology of New England* (New York: Hill and Wang, 1983), 146; Strausbaugh and Core, 108.

42. See Strausbaugh and Core, viii.

43. Davis, 178.

44. Strother, 'Virginia Canaan,' 25. *The Blackwater Chronicle* contains similar passages.

45. Strother, 'Virginia Canaan,' 26.

46. *Fairfax Line*, 46.

47. Davis, 179.

48. I have not been able to confirm Kennedy's description of these 'salmon-colored' trout. No other early source describes the fish of the Blackwater in any detail. Robert Barnwell Roosevelt's 1862 *Game Fish of the Northern States of America* (rpt. New York: Arno Press, 1967), a standard nineteenth-century reference, does not note any such color variant; the 'Red Trout' mentioned here is evidently a land-locked salmon (13).

49. Strother, 'The Mountains—VII,' 676. Davis gives a similar description, 178. On the 'forest fallow' or 'backwoods'

method of agriculture common in the region, see Ronald L. Lewis, *Transforming the Appalachian Countryside: Railroads, Deforestation, and Social Change in West Virginia, 1880-1920* (Chapel Hill: University of North Carolina Press, 1998), 19-35; Terry G. Jordan and Matti Kaups, *The American Backwoods Frontier: An Ethnic and Ecological Interpretation* (Baltimore: Johns Hopkins University Press, 1990).

50. See Lewis, especially 71-72, 92-94, 143-46; Homer Floyd Fansler, *History of Tucker County, West Virginia* (Parsons, W. Va.: McClain Printing Co., 1962), 446, 464-66, 533, 546, 549, 578, 582, quote taken from 466. For a brief overview of logging operations in the region, see Jack Waugh, 'Lumbering Before Pinchot,' *American Heritage* 42 (Feb./Mar. 1991): 93-96.

51. I wish to thank Todd Petty, West Virginia University Division of Forestry, for providing information on the environmental impact of logging and mining in the region.

52. Today, some ancient hemlocks remain in a 132-acre stand of old-growth mixed forest in Cathedral State Park near Aurora. A 50-acre stand of old-growth red spruce survives in the Gaudineer Scenic Area of the Monongahela National Forest.

53. Strother's sketches for 'The Virginia Canaan' would take advantage of the larger, two-column layout of *Harper's Magazine* to expand the artistic possibilities of landscape representation while maintaining his characteristic social focus.

54. I wish to thank Harold Forbes, West Virginia and Regional History Collection, who reproduced the images and consulted on other matters.

THE

BLACKWATER CHRONICLE

A NARRATIVE OF AN EXPEDITION INTO

THE LAND OF CANAAN,

IN RANDOLPH COUNTY, VIRGINIA,

A COUNTRY FLOWING WITH WILD ANIMALS, SUCH AS PANTHERS,
BEARS, WOLVES, ELK, DEER, OTTER, BADGER, &c., &c., WITH
INNUMERABLE TROUT — BY FIVE ADVENTUROUS GENTLE-
MEN, WITHOUT ANY AID OF GOVERNMENT, AND SOLELY
BY THEIR OWN RESOURCES, IN THE SUMMER OF 1851.

By "The Clerke of Oxenforde."

WITH ILLUSTRATIONS FROM LIFE BY STROTHER.

REDFIELD
110 AND 112 NASSAU STREET, NEW YORK.
1853.

CHAPTER I.

INTRODUCTORY.

—◆—

I<small>F</small> the reader will take down the map of Virginia, and look at Randolph county, he will find that the Blackwater is a stream that makes down from the north into the Cheat river, some few miles below the point where that river is formed by the junction of the Dry fork, the Laurel fork, and the Glade fork—the Shavers, or Great fork, falling in some miles below: all rising and running along the western side of the Backbone of the Alleganies.

The country embraced by these head-waters of the Cheat river is called "The Canaan"—a wilderness of broken and rugged mountains—its streams falling through deep clefts, or leaping down in great cataracts, into the Cheat, that sweeps the base of the Backbone.

It is to the Blackwater, one among the largest of these streams of the Canaan, that we purpose to take the reader. If, therefore, his fancy urges him to the venture, let him come with us. All he has to do is to set himself down in his easy-chair, and lend us his ears. By the magic of this scroll we shall take him.

This Blackwater (it should be called Amberwater), and north source of the Cheat, rises high up on the western slope of the Backbone, directly across from the Fairfax stone—where the head-spring of the Potomac has its source on this the eastern side of the mountain; and it is supposed that these headwaters of the two rivers are not more than some half a mile (or mile at most) apart. The Backbone, following a general course from north to south, here turns at almost a right-angle, and takes across to the eastward some fifteen miles, when it regains its former southerly direction, thus forming a zigzag in its course. At the point where it first makes the bend to the east, a large spur—apparently the Backbone itself—keeps straight to the south, and butts down on the Cheat, at the distance of some ten or twelve miles. Between this large spur and the point where the Backbone bends to the south again, is contained the cove of mountains which is called the Canaan. This region of country is in the very highest range of the Alleganies, lying in the main some three thousand feet above the level of the sea.

Until a few years past, the whole of the district embraced by the head-waters of the Potomac and the Cheat was as remote and inaccessible as any part of the long range of the Alleganies. But some few years ago, the state of Virginia constructed a graded road from Winchester to Parkersburg, which passes over the Backbone through the Potomac limits; and consequently this portion of the district has become opened out somewhat to the knowledge of the world, and has since been settled to a considerable extent. The Baltimore and Ohio railroad also passes near here—at a distance from the head-waters of the Potomac varying from ten to twenty miles. The railroad will bring all this region within a day's travel of the seaboard; and as the country lies about the head of the Maryland glades—in themselves a source of attraction—and contains within its range many tracts of land of great fertility and beauty, it is not irrational to suppose that it will be cleared out and settled with rapidity.

As it is, there is a good settlement around here already—the result, in the main, of the construction of the Northwestern road. Long, however, before this road was made, there was a Mr. Smith who pitched his tent in these wilds some fifty years or more ago, I am informed, and cleared out and improved a handsome estate for himself, lying along the Maryland shore of the Potomac, and containing some fifteen hundred acres of fine land of varied hill and dale. The Smiths are now gone, and the estate has passed into other hands. In the older times a tavern was kept here, for the accommodation of the few people who crossed these mountains. But when the Northwestern road came by, the marvels of a good highway were made manifest in the increased travel, that soon became too great for the capabilities of the once-unfriended inn. About this period, a gentleman from the city of Washington, journeying this way to escape the heats of the seaboard, was so taken with the pleasant temperature of the air and the wild beauty of the mountains, that he bought the place—impelled somewhat thereto, no doubt, by the trout in the streams and the deer in the forests. Under his rule a new house was erected, large enough to hold a goodly company. This is the house—fair enough to look upon in its outside array, and comfortable enough within—that now stands imposing, not far away from the old one, on the brow of a lofty hill overlooking the Potomac. "Winston" the place is called—so called because the eighty-seventh milestone from Winchester is won when you reach its door. Edward Towers keeps it—or did, when the Blackwater expedition won the stone. Here, for some years past, many of our citizens, of both Virginia and Maryland, have been in the habit of resorting in the summer and fall months, to fish for trout, hunt the deer, shoot pheasants, wild turkeys, woodcock in their season, and enjoy the invigorating atmosphere of a country whose level is so high above the sea.

The ride to this place over the Northwestern road is exquisitely delightful, and withal as easy as a ride can well be. You travel over a graded slate road—the perfection of a summer highway—engineered skillfully, and at but a low grade, through the gorges and defiles of these fine mountains, and, when crossing any of them, seeming to have been carried over purposely at those points where the scenery is of the grandest or most beautiful character. Take it altogether, for the excellence of the road, and the varied combinations of scenery that are ever presenting themselves to view, there is no route across the mountains anywhere that excels it. With a pair of good horses in a light carriage, you can speed along all the way as if you were taking an evening drive about your home, even though your home be where the roads are the best in the land. And then, what exhilaration of spirit is felt by you as you roll smoothly along at the rate of some ten miles an hour, your horses scarcely stretching a trace—seeming merely to keep out of the way of the wheels!—on one side of you a deep gorge, a thousand feet down, dark with hemlocks and firs, where a mountain-stream breaks its way to the sea; above you, high-towering peaks and over-hanging cliffs, where the oak or stately fir has cast anchor, and held on for ages in defiance of all the storms of the Alleganies; while before you, afar off, glittering in the sunshine, are seen in glimpses the green fields and meadows of some fair, luxuriant valley; and the whole horizon bounded by lofty mountains that seem to defy all approach, but which you at length wind your way through by some concealed cleft, the bed of a stream, with scarcely any more of obstruction than a bowling-green would present to your glowing wheels.

There are but few things more agreeably exciting to the spirits than a rapid drive through the country on a good road. There are some who will not assent to this proposition; but they are not to be deferred to in these matters of *fastness*, and do not understand the philosophy of the human soul. "The power of agitation upon the spirits," says Dr. Johnson, "is well known. Every man has felt his heart lightened by a rapid drive or a gallop on a swift horse." This might be only a little closet philosophy of the sturdy old despot of letters, maintained in theory but belied in practice, like our famous doctrine of state-rights here in Virginia; but we have it on record that the rough old viking of our English literature considered it one of the prime felicities of his life to ride in a stage-coach, even at the rate of speed attainable in his day. If one of the soundest moral philosophers that any age or country has produced can be shown as both theoretically and practically enforcing the happiness of rapid motion—at least to the extent that could be achieved by an English stage-coach, and over the comparatively rude thoroughfares leading out of London a hundred years ago—*ante Agamemnona*, that is, before M'Adam—how much more delightful must be the agitation of your spirits, and the consequent lightening of your heart, when the atmosphere you breathe, as you drive smoothly along behind a pair of untiring thoroughbreds, is the very purest, and the scenes around you are among the grandest or most beautiful of a whole continent! And all this too, recollect, with a splendid craving all over you—feeling it even at your finger-ends—everywhere—for food: visions of venison-steaks, and hot rolls, and fresh summer butter, made where the meadows are "with daisies pied," floating through your crowded and hunger-enraptured brain—and with the certainty, too, all the while in your mind, that you can not apparently kill this craving for the time being with anything in the shape of a breakfast, dinner, supper, or what not, but it will be all powerful again upon you in some three or four hours!—an appetite seemingly endowed with the quality of the phoenix, that out of its own ashes renews itself—

> ——"revives and flourishes,
> Like that self-begotten bird,
> In the Arabian woods embossed"—

not surpassed by anything of the sort that we have on record—not by Sancho Panza's, nor by Rittmaster Dugald Dalgetty's, nor yet that of the mighty heroes of the Iliad—aptly to describe which the genius of Homer was only equal, when the divine old bard sings of it as the *sacred rage of hunger.*

If any mortal of these sated days would wish fully to appreciate what this Homeric rage is, let him take this ride to the Alleganies; and though he should be of a nobler spirit than Esau, yet will he in his inmost soul commiserate that poor devil for having sold his birthright for a mess of pottage.

WHITNEY—JOCELYN—ANNIN. SC

CHAPTER II.

GETTING UNDER WAY.

＊‡＊

> "The stout earl of Northumberland
>   A vow to God did make,
>   His pleasure on the Scottish ground
>   Three summer days to take."

THE stout Earl Percy, here alluded to, did take his pleasure on the Scottish ground—and how, all the world knows that has read the fine old ballad of "Chevy Chase." How the stout gentlemen, and also those who were none of the stoutest, who took their pleasure on the Blackwater, came off, hearken to the following chronicle, and you shall learn.

It was toward the first of June last past, that a number of gentlemen, residing near each other, in a pleasant part of that rich valley vaunted to the world as *the garden of Virginia*, and called by the people of the mountain-ranges back of it *the land of Egypt*, from the quantity of grain which it produces, determined to make a pleasure expedition into the Allegany country, having it chiefly in view to harry its streams for trout. Accordingly, on one fine morning—it was on the last day of the universally-lauded month of May—we gathered together, prepared as best we knew how for the expedition.

It was at the pleasant country-dwelling of Mr. Peter Botecote, one of our number, that we made our rendezvous:—

> "And Wat of Harden came thither amain,
> And thither came John of Thirlestane,
> And thither came William of Deloraine"—

and all the rest of us—men, dogs, and horses. Here, after some animated parley, and an early dinner, it was resolved that we should forthwith take our departure, notwithstanding the strawberries that were ripe in the garden, and the cream that was abounding in the dairy, and what too was far more delaying, the fascination of our lady-hostess. Pleasant enough this bower of Botecote's; but hope smiled its enchantments upon us far away, from the very midst of the wild Alleganies, and our hearts were too much agog and all a-tiptoe with its illusions, to think of staying. The delirium of the mountains was upon us; and so, amid the neighing and pawing of horses, the speeding to and fro of servants, the dancing eyes of children, and the wife's half-sorrowful smile as she committed her adventurous husband to the destiny of a two or three weeks' separation, we wheeled into order, and took up the line of march. "Hey!"—"Get away!"—"Ho!"—"Ha, you dog!"—whips flourishing, dogs barking—all the commotion that a country-gentleman's establishment could well get up; every good spirit attending, to say nothing of the high ones: thus we left the Botecote portals, and—

"All the blue bonnets are over the border!"

We drove to Winchester, a town when George II. was king here in Virginia: not one of your recent cities, grown up to a hundred thousand people within the memory of men alive, but an old, time-honored town, of some five thousand souls, with remembrances about it; familiar to the footsteps of Thomas, the sixth Lord Fairfax, when he lived at Greenway court (some ten miles off), and held power as lieutenant of the county of Frederick, hunted the boar, wrote for "The Spectator," and set twenty covers daily at his table: famous, too, in our provincial history, as the military headquarters of Washington during the war of '65 against the French for the possession of the western country. Here, to this old border stronghold of the Dominion, where the dismantled ramparts of Fort Loudon still look down upon the town, we drove over night, a matter of some twenty miles, ready to make a more sustained movement the next morning on Winston—some eighty-seven miles distant, as already stated, on the Northwestern road.

The expedition travelled in three light carriages, such as are commonly called *wagons*, all tight and sound, freshly washed, oiled, and rubbed, and glittering in the sun "like images:" each wagon drawn by a vigorous trotter in fine condition, and able on a good road easily to make such time as would have satisfied Dr. Johnson, even though his philosophy of happiness should have required a greater speed than ten miles an hour. We were five in all: the sixth didn't go, that gentleman having failed us by the way, owing to some anxieties he entertained about trusting himself so high up on the continent. But no matter; we were yet five. There was—

Mr. Peter Botecote, generally called Butcut by his familiars—sometimes But;

Mr. Guy Philips, the Master of the priory of St. Philips: hence familiarly the master, sometimes the Prior, and occasionally "the county Guy;"

Triptolemus Todd, Esq., our Murad the Unlucky, and sometimes Trip;

Doctor Adolphus Blandy, physician to the expedition: Galen he was called for short;

And the Signor Andante Strozzi, our artist, also amateur musician.

Mr. Perry Winkle, jocosely called by his friends, in one syllable, *Perrywinkle*, is the name of the gentleman who *didn't* go—which we mention here that he may not altogether escape immortality—and would also give his likeness, were it not for a well-founded apprehension that it might too much divert the attention of the reader from our narrative.

The array, it will be perceived from the naming, is somewhat imposing, and gives promise of something to be done and said out of the common. Truly, this record of the performance need not fall short of the promise, if the ambitious chronicler can succeed, by any happy art, in anything like a history that shall be a just impress—an impress of the body and soul—of the expedition. Thucydides hit it, in his narrative of *The Sailing for Sicily*, also in *The Landing of Alcibiades at Athens*; Livy, in that part of his twenty-first book which we've got, and no doubt in the remainder of it, if we could only find it; Segur, in the retreat from Moscow; Macaulay, in the landing of the prince of Orange, and the march on London; Voltaire's Charles the Twelfth, too, ought not to be passed over in this enumeration; nor yet Sallust's little narrative of Catiline. Let us add another to the illustrious roll, by writing the Blackwater Narrative up to the immortal standard.

Deserted, then, by Mr. Perrywinkle, we were yet five in number; all good men and true, and of unusually diversified character and appearance: none of us to be called old in years, but old enough in the ups and downs, and ins and outs of this world, having made "many hair-breadth 'scapes by flood and field," by town and country, by man and woman also, in our time—even the more youthful Triptolemus, who has killed in his time several good pointers in shooting partridges, and some few years ago shot himself in the right knee—which will account for his lameness in these pages. Without mincing matters too much, we will speak it out freely, that we were all men of some mark and likelihood, as men go; and although the world might not judge us (which it is our opinion it would make a great mistake in not doing) as "fit to stand by Caesar in a tented field," there can be no doubt that it would hold us all, if it had the honor of our acquaintance, as fit to sit by that "foremost man of all the world," at a dinner or a supper, at any rate.

We will take the liberty of saying, however, with great modesty, and begging pardon of everybody, and especially of the old Romans, that if "the mightiest Julius" had been along with us upon this expedition, he would have found the passage into the country of the Blackwater a far more fatiguing enterprise than any of his incursions into the countries of the Allobrogi, or Nervii, or Acquitanii, or Boii, or any other of those outsiders, against whom the elegant and captivating greatest Roman marched.

It will not be amiss here to mention, that we travelled upon our inroad very much after the fashion in which Caesar went upon his. Grave History has not thought it beneath her dignity to record how the great master of the Roman world went upon his depredations; and it is one of her condescensions for which we are very much obliged to her. It is therefore, we know, among other things of this elegant and all-accomplished subverter of the republic and founder of the fourth and last universal empire, that he rode in a carriage upon his forays. This carriage was called a *rheda*, "a sort of gig or curricle," says a recent very distinguished authority, Mr. De Quincey, "a four-wheeled carriage, and adapted to the conveyance of about half a ton." This, the reader will perceive, is in and about our modern wagon; and we have no doubt, if the matter were fairly investigated, it would be ascertained that the rheda of the Roman is the prototype of the wagon of the American: it's a four-runner at any rate. Julius used this carriage, we are informed, because it enabled him to take with him the amount of equipment that was essential to his elegant and patrician habits: his various mantles—for instance, the one he overcame the Nervii in, which he preserved and wore many years after in the city, and was the same in which the envious Casca made the rent, that Shakspere and Casca between them have made so immortal; his bandboxes, in which he kept the wreaths he wore around his head, as our ladies do now on festival occasions—the ivy, the laurel, the oak wreaths, and what others I know not; his bathing apparatus, brushes, soaps, &c.; his unguents and perfumes, with the various ancient Roman balms for the cure of baldness. The rheda was adjusted to the convenient transportation of these essentials of an elegant Roman gentleman of that day: and so the wagon to the wants of the daintiest gentleman of this.

It will be perceived, therefore, that our expedition has many points of resemblance to those so famous of the splendid Roman. It was depredatory in the first place. It combined, in the second, about an equal commingling of the luxurious and the rough-and-tumble. Thirdly: considering that it took the field about nineteen centuries later than Caesar's, there is a very remarkable resemblance between the vehicles used in both. Fourthly: in one single engagement, fought on the Blackwater, and which lasted only about two hours, no less than four hundred and ninety some odd of the enemy were slain, and what is more, fully a hundred of them eaten next thing to alive: and this, we take it, will compare with anything done in Gaul. Lastly: the wild tribes that infested the Alleganies, fled before our arms; many a flying army of deer owed their lives to the mercy of the invaders; the badgers and the otters—a feeble people, yet sagacious and wary—we laid ourselves out to take by policy, that is entrap them, as Caesar did the like people of Gaul; and had not the fierce panthers, the rude bears, the prowling wolves, and the other warlike inhabitants of these untamed forests, betaken themsleves to their fastnesses, and there remained with a savage fortitude that defied hunger all the time we were out, we should have vanquished them with as great slaughter as befell the Boii, and Nervii, the Helvetians, the Acquitanii, Vercingetorix, Orgetorix, Dumnorix, Benorix, and all the other Orixes, at the hand of Julius—roasted and devoured some of them too, next thing to alive.

But enough. The reader is, no doubt, by this time, impressed with a due sense of the dignity of our undertaking. Let us not then any longer dally with our narrative, but hasten on to the field of our renown.

CHAPTER III.

IN WHICH THE EXPEDITION DANCES A HORNPIPE ON THE TOP OF A MOUNTAIN.

A FTER an early breakfast at about sunrise, we left the hotel in Winchester on the morning of the 1st of June; and taking out the Northwestern road, we went on our way rejoicing. Passing through the North mountain, five miles out, where it breaks down almost on a level with the valley we had just left, we entered fairly into the mountain region—whence it is nothing but chain after chain, until you cross over the broad belt to the great, spreading, western, shining plain, watered by the Mississippi and its tributaries.

For several hours we traveled along without stint or stay, filled with the bliss of this first morning of June. Our horses tread the ground lightly, vigorous and nimble-footed, no touch of weariness yet upon them; and our swift wheels turn with scarce-perceptible sound—a mere low hum along the slaty road. Delicious is the summer's day, delicious to both soul and sense! No poet's dream of June was ever so enchanting. It has rained over night, and fresh and fragrant everywhere is the morning. The forest-leaves are all washed clean as the waters of heaven can make them, and the grasses are more delicately green in their renewal. The rain-drops, not yet dried up, sparkle all over the forest, in the glittering sunshine, like beads of pearl. All nature, animate and inanimate—on four legs, two, or none—feels the heavenly influence of the hour. The woods are vocal with the rapturous voice of birds. The wild-flowers—the wild-rose and the wood-violet, the gorgeous laurel, and the sweet elder-bloom—in all their freshened glory, give their delicate perfumes to the liberal air, and their hues of heaven to the enraptured sight. The streams, sometimes crossing our path, and sometimes flowing on by our side—seeming to go with us whichever way we go—flowing on adown the dell or by the rifted rock, and all embowered with shrubs and tangled vines: these sing their sweet songs tuneful to the ear, until at length, ecstasy—born of the murmuring waters, the balm of the air, the glory of the wild-flowers, the warble of the birds, and the smooth velocity of your rheda—enters into the heart, and pervades your countenance with a radiance that is almost divine.

Thus full of all joy that is born of summer and the mountains, we speed on our way—to happiness and to Winston! On we drive, over the smooth road, through gorge, and dell, and valley, when by-and-by we ascend a mountain, winding up its side like the track of a snake, until we reach the top. Here a magnificent panorama of distant-blending valleys and mountains piled on mountains, breaks suddenly on our view; and, seized with a shouting spirit of exultation—

> "We call a halt, and make a stand,
> And cry, 'St. George for merry England!' "—

meaning thereby this all-hailed land of ours, which the patriotic reader will of course understand.

The day is now some four hours old by the shadow; and before yet the last echoes of our voices have died away in the hills and rocks around, a wayfarer, all in minstrel array bedight, walked in wearily among us. *He* called a halt, and made a stand, too, on the mountain's brow. This was a wandering Italian, with his hand-organ strapped to his back, who had ascended from the other side; and it was not long before he had unburdened himself of his bread-winner, and given us a specimen of what his art could do. His instrument was a very good one, and our imaginations had by this time thrown around him an air of romance and poetry. Had we encountered him in the streets of a city, he would have been nothing more than an ordinary strolling minstrel to us; but here, in the forest, his music struck upon the ear pleasantly enough, and brought to its aid much poetic association. It sounded of the days when the old harper begged his bread from door to door: and the hand-organ is already half-elevated into the harp, and he who turns it has a soul alive to poetry and song. Happy power of illusion! it is better than gold in gilding this bare life—this life so bare and hard to the pure reason, so full of charm to the imagination!

Thus idealizing the hand-organ and the very good-looking, rather handsome man, who turned it, we now left our wagons; and, out in the road, and face to face, we hold friendly parley with the stranger. The wandering minstrel is a Neapolitan; and the Singor Strozzi, our artist, glad of a chance to refresh himself with a little Italian, immediately enlarges upon the renowned city—its towers and palaces, the bay, the towns around, and the neighboring volcano lurid in the heavens. Not unmindful of his country, there is moisture in the eye of the minstrel, and something very like a tear is on his cheek. There is something sympathetic in all show of feeling; and when the prior of St. Philips repeated in feeling tones the song of the harper in Rokeby—

> "Wo came with war, and want with wo,
> And it was mine to undergo
> Each outrage of the rebel foe:
>   Can aught atone
> My fields laid waste, my cot laid low?
>   My harp alone!
>
> "Ambition's dreams I've seen depart,
> Have rued of penury the smart,
> Have felt of love the venomed dart,

When hope was flown;
Yet rests one solace to my heart—
My harp alone!

"Then o'er mountain, moor, and hill,
My faithful harp, I'll bear thee still,
And when this life of want and ill
Is well nigh gone,
Thy strings mine elegy shall thrill,
My harp alone!"—

when the feeling prior, here on the mountain's brow, crooned forth these verses—the ruined exile standing tired before him, with his arm thrown over his bread-winner—let the susceptibility to emotion be here recorded of the expedition, which made us draw forth our purses and give to this rude votary of the "joyous science" more silver and gold than he had gathered in a week in all his roaming. We were as good as two or three villages to him.

Having, however, some latent, half shame-prompted idea that we might be indulging a little too much in a sentimental luxury, incompatible with the manly and somewhat rough, Runic character of our enterprise, we daffed aside these softer emotions, and struck off into a lighter and gayer strain, more in keeping with the actual state of the case around us. And so the Neapolitan, Jacomo, assumed once more his usual professional bearing, and struck his lyre to the strains that nightly over the earth swell the hearts of those who worship at the feet of Terpsichore—that is, he played us some waltzes and polkas. And presently we all began to dance—the little figures in the glass case in front of the organ, and we on the slaty summit of the mountain-road. Away we go, in fine accord with the minstrelsey— now waltzing together in bold sweeps around the brow of the mountain; and now, with arms akimbo, dancing a polka, in many mazy gyrations, after the most approved manner of executing that dance, as it was first exhibited by the ballet-people at our theatres, before yet it became fashionable in high life. The whole affair we concluded with *Fisher's hornpipe*, through which we capered with such surprising agility as was never before or since made manifest on the top of any mountain in the United States—

or, probably, at the bottom of any one either. As we danced, we all sang, too, in accompaniment with the strains, thus doubly taxing our powers. The dust flew, and rose into the heavens; Jacomo's black eye sparkled as he swiftly turned his crank. The scene was as intense as the race down the quarter stretch between Eclipse and Henry, when North and South hung suspended on the strife. We swam the very air agile and swift-bounding—some of us—as the antelope; others with a strained, incongruous jerking and ponderous agility, very much like what might be supposed of a buffalo in a hornpipe. Even the lame leg of Murad the Unlucky might be caught a glimpse of, every now and then, flying about in the midst of the hurly-burly as something independent of anybody present: in our American vernacular, it seemed to be *going it on its own hook*. The horses drew up around us with their wagons, and, with ears bent forward, and fascinated gaze, looked on in pleased wonderment. *Fisher's hornpipe* is perhaps one of the fastest tunes now known in all Christendom; and yet, fast as we danced it, we sang it. It was thus the wild descant rang through the forest:—

> "Did you ever see the devil,
> With his iron wooden shovel,
> A scratching up the gravel,
> With his nightcap on?
>
> "No, I never saw the devil,
> With his iron wooden shovel,

A scratching up the gravel,
With his nightcap on."
[*Repeated twice.*]

"Did you ever, ever, ever,
Ever, ever, ever, ever,
Ever, ever, ever, ever,
Catch a whale by the tail?

"No, I never, never, never,
Never, never, never, never,
Never, never, never, never,
Caught a whale by the tail."
[*Repeated twice.*]

The echoes around take up our voices at every pause for breath; the mountains, as in the old Bible times, cry aloud for joy; and *ever see the devil*, and *nightcap on*, and *whale by the tail*, in the cadence of the hornpipe, are repeated far and near, until at length the uproar dies away—in some far remote dell, a last faint, feeble sound of *whale . . . tail*, lingering for a moment on the ear, and all is hushed: the echoes have gone to sleep again, and nothing breaks upon the stillness of the mountains, save the lazy sound of the summer wind, that is itself almost silence.

Somewhat fagged and out of breath, we now once more took to our wagons, the horses by this time well rested; and leaving the Neapolitan, disconsolate Jacomo, standing irresolute on the mountain's brow, we swept down the windings of the highway, at the rate of some twelve miles to the hour—Jacomo still standing motionless as a picture, as we entered a wild defile of the forest, and for ever lost him to the sight. Winding our way over a broken range of picturesque hills, we at length entered a ravine, down which a clear, sparkling stream hunts its course to a neighboring river. Here are some very remarkable cliffs of a pure white sandstone, which is in some demand among the nicer housekeepers of Winchester and Romney for scouring purposes. Into the base of one of these cliffs, a large excavation has been made, where the rock is so purely white, that it suggests to you the idea of a quarry of the finest loaf-sugar. Passing these loaf-sugar cliffs, we drove on leisurely down the cool ravine, by the banks and through the fords of the silvery stream, when presently we emerged from the deep shadows of some thickly-clustered hemlocks and pines into the light of day, and found ourselves before the tavern door of Mr. Charles Blue. Here we stopped to feed and rest our horses for some two or three hours—taking care, in the meantime, to regale ourselves with such delicacies of fried chickens, broiled ham and eggs, and fresh butter and milk, as the house afforded us.

About two o'clock—the day being still pleasant, and without any burdensome heat—we took to the road again; and after some two hours' travel, through the green valleys and over other mountains, we at length came in sight of the little town of Romney, beautifully situated upon a sloping plateau of land that lies back of the high banks and bluffs of the

South Branch; the river here flowing along in all its winding lines of beauty—on through rich bottoms and bold over-hanging mountains, to its junction with the Potomac.

Somewhere about four o'clock—after descending a long and beautiful sweep of road, grand enough in all its features to be the avenue to some lordly city—we drove up to the door of the village inn (the old Virginia designation is ordinary), situated pleasantly on the main street of Romney, and kept by Mr. Armstrong, formerly a member of Congress from this district, but who has for some years past chosen the better part—shaken the dust of the capitol from his feet, and commanded the respect and good will of all considerate people who travel this way, by the manner in which he discharges his present representative duty to the public. In this comfortable inn, we took our ease for the rest of the day, having accomplished just forty-four miles over those mountains, since we first drew rein in the morning.

How the Signor Strozzi was taken by some of the good people of Romney for an Italian revolutionist—how Doctor Blandy built a very remarkable castle in the air, that from a neighboring eminence commanded the South Branch valley—how Mr. Butcut set the porch in a roar, at a story he told of some cockneys who came over to New York to hunt bears about that city; how the Prior discoursed eloquently on Lucerne grass and the ancients; how Triptolemus, when the levée we held on the porch was at the highest, called everybody by somebody else's name; how we passed altogether a very cheerful and gay evening of it, among the social citizens of Romney, who did us the honor to make our acquaintance—we will not detain the reader by setting forth in full in these pages, but here end this chapter, and with it the narrative of the evening.

CHAPTER IV.

THE COCKNEYS EXPLAINED BY THE PRIOR OF ST. PHILIPS, FROM THE TOP OF THE ALLEGANY.

W<small>HAT</small> time the skylark plumed his wing, the expedition awoke from its slumbers, and betimes arose; what time the sun peeped into the casements of the village hostel, it sat triumphant over a routed breakfast-table, and, like Alexander, sighed that it had no more to conquer. In this condition, he of Macedon took to drink—but we to our wagons, with a good-by to pleasant Romney.

The morning was delightfully bracing. Whether it was the mountain-air, or the mountain-oats, that inspired them, our horses carried themselves as proud as reindeers, and went down the main street of Romney with a free swing, fully up to the requirements of the Dr. Johnson philosophy in this matter. As we crossed the high plain to the bluffs of the river, the scenery of the South-Branch valley was just developing into expression—the mountain in bold masses, the winding river with its mists, the rich bottoms striped with cornfields, the long range of brown cliffs in the distance, and in the foreground the high plain on which sat the picturesque town: all in striking contrasts of light and shade; the dark shadows of the mountains, and the golden mists of the river; the spangled dewdrops on the meadows, and the funeral drapery of the pine-forests; Apollo, from his chariot of the sun, elimning some new glory of the picture, as he drove on up the steeps of the skies.

This glimpse of the sunrise-picture was all we saw, for it is but a mile from the town to the bluffs of the river, and these we have already gained. We now descended from the table-land, and crossed the South Branch by a good bridge. With the river on one side and the overhanging mountain on the other, we drove on for a mile or so; when we turned off, and passed through the mountain on almost a dead-level road, winding along the side of a stream that here makes its way through a deep cleft to the river. For some fifteen miles the road is a beautiful one—smooth, and of easy grade in its gradual rise toward the Alleganies; now hugging the hills, now following the bends of the streams, now through valleys spotted with farmhouses and green with luxuriant grass. At length we came to the Knobley, which we ascended, passing through a hamlet scattered carelessly along the cultivated slopes of the mountain. This mountain presents a very remarkable outline, being a succession of high knobs or peaks with intervening low depressions, giving it the appearance of an indented castle-wall. Through one of these depressions we crossed, and descended by easy traverses to the other side. For a mile or so we wound our way through the defiles of a broken range of hills, and emerged at length into a narrow and beautifully-picturesque valley—the Allegany piled up in grand masses on one side, and the road running for some miles along the banks of a clear, rapid stream, known hereabouts as New creek—just such a stream, so wild and cool, as the imagination would fill with trout a foot and a quarter long, and some four inches deep behind the shoulders.

By the side of the sparkling creek, with (no doubt) trout to be had for the casting of a fly, or the impaling of a worm, we found a large and comfortable brick house, where a Mr. Reese keeps an inn highly spoken of in these parts for its excellent accommodations. At the base of the Allegany stands invitingly the mountain-embowered inn. In front of this is the clear, cool, wild, dancing stream; and up beyond this again, rises with bold ascent, almost at right-angles to the water, a richly-wooded spur of the Allegany, colored with all-blended hues of green, from the pale tea-color of the mountain-ash, to the dark, grand, gloom green, almost invisible green, of the clustered fir-trees and hemlocks—these the nobler pines that more particularly distinguish the forests of the Allegany ranges.

From Reese's house, at the base, it is seven miles to the top of the Allegany—something of an Olympus to the warts behind us. Mindful of our horses, we gird up our loins for the encounter, and take to the heaven-kissing hill afoot. Half-way up there is a fountain of pure spring-water caught in a rude trough by the roadside; and men and horses gather around, and revel in the mountain hippocrene. The lookout from here is already grand. Far and wide you behold the land we have traveled. On we go again, up and up, still up; and the air you breathe is freer, and the scene wilder and yet more widely revealed at every turn of the road, rounding each rocky promontory that juts the mountain-side.

In something more than two hours we reached the toll-gate, situated near the summit of the ridge, and commanding a prospect of all the land lying abroad to the eastward. This is one of the grandest and most diversified mountain-scenes in the whole range of our country: mountains piled on mountains everywhere, of every variety of size and shape, with all their valleys, glens, gorges, dells, and narrow defiles—all yet varied by the changing light and shade that falls upon them from the heavens—as the heavens are ablaze with sunshine, or swept by passing summer-clouds.

Altogether it is such a scene as seldom meets the eye. At once its glory has entered into the heart and fired the imagination, and we are a thousand times over repaid for the long, toilsome ascent that has given it to us. To view it aright, it should be seen under all changing aspects: at the dawn and the sunrise; under the earlier and the later shadows of the morning; when the midday blaze has made it all dreamy as an ocean unmoved; as the shadows lengthen upon it in the evening; as the gloom of the twilight gathers over it. To see it in its greatest sublimity, you should be here when, bare of leaf, and all rugged in its disclosure, it is terrible with the howling storms of winter—storms sweeping dreadfully both the heavens and the earth!

Yet, even in a half-hour's glance, much will be written upon the mind that can never be effaced; and this "dim spot, that men call earth," will be ever after greatly dignified to your appreciation. A scene thus ennobling, let us not pass away from it too lightly. Let us portray it, even though it be with such indistinct limning as the few moments we loitered at the toll gate will enable.

You are at such height here at the gate, that as you stand looking eastward, there is nothing to bound your vision but your natural horizon. You are above the whole scene; and looking over it, you may be said to look down over it. You command it all, to the extent of the power of the eye. Far below you, some thousands of feet, is a wood-embosomed dell, with an open farm every here and there spotted along it, looking at this distance like patches of wild meadow and glade in the midst of the vast forest around. Immediately beyond rises a bold and rugged mountain, whose craggy top is indented like the battlements of a castle, and whose sides sweep down, dark with firs and hemlocks, and every variety of pines, to the edge of the deep valley. Looking to the right, the mountains are broken and irregular, as if they had been tossed and torn to pieces by some mighty upheaving of the earth, and had thus fallen scattered about in confused, giant masses: some elegant and majestic as the "star'y-pointed pyramid;" some grand and massive as the "proud bulwark on the steep;" others of huge, misshapen bulk—the Calibans of the wild; and others, again, so grotesque of form, that they seem to have been moulded by the very genius of Whim—the Merry-Andrews of the Alleganies: and all yet beautiful and soft to the eye, with the softening hues of summer—these summer hues producing the same effect here that time has wrought upon the rugged feudal castle, as so beautifully described in the verse of Mason:—

> ——"Time
> Has moulded into beauty many a tower,
> Which, when it frowned with all its battlements,
> Was only terrible"——

On the left the scene is in strong contrast with the grand and grotesque mountains we have just described. Here, along the steeps of the Allegany, you catch picturesque glimpses of the winding highway—and, again, you see it boldly emerging from the woods at the base of the mountain, and sweeping on through the open vale, and by the banks of the silvery stream, down past the embowered house and cultivated lands of Reese—on—and away, until it turns off, and is lost in the mountains. This little valley, which but this morning we traversed in part, now stretches itself out so far before us that it grows indistinct and confused to the sight—its fields so diminished in size that they look like garden-beds; the winding stream that threads it seeming but a waving line of silver. The picture has all the delicacy of a scene in miniature, and there is a witching summer-softness over it all as of the beauty and the sheen of a voluptuous woman, or (if you prefer it) of a ripe peach. Further over in the mountains is a wider and more open valley, that seems from here almost a plain, and so hazy and indistinct are its outlines, that your imagination exerts its fanciful power, and you see—dimly—vaguely—towers, and temples, and mighty domes, revealing themselves before your eyes, as if some lordly city was about to grow up upon the plain by enchantment. Turning again, and looking straight forward, eastwardly, whence we came, and lo! what ideas of vastness crowd upon the mind; for it is all one vast sea of mountains, as far as the eye can behold—range beyond range ever appearing— heaving like the blue waves of some immense sea— wave following wave in endless succession; for your horizon being bounded everywhere by mountains, to the imagination there is no limit, and all beyond is wave after wave of the same giant sea.

Gazing upon this noble scene, the prior of St. Philips grew excited—his eye dilated—his soul was all ablaze; and no longer able to hold himself, he stretched forth his right hand and gave tongue as follows:—

"Gentlemen, I see into it all now, and if our invasion of the Alleganies effects nothing else I shall go home satisfied. Our mountains have been greatly slandered—most vilely traduced by the cockneys; and beholding this mighty scene, I'm lost in wonder that some man with a large enough soul, hasn't long since put them right before the world."

"That's right, stick it into them, Prior; give it to 'em, County, you're the man to do it."

"Put to route and everlasting shame the whole insolent and conceited herd."

> "Hash them, slash them,
> All to pieces dash them!"

"Let them have it as Tom Hyer gave it to Sulivan."

"Dress their jackets genteely, Prior."

"Don't spare either age, sex, or condition."

"Begin:—

> "'Omnes conticuere intentique ora tenebant,
> Sic—'"

"*Sic* who! He don't want any sicking, let him go on."

Silence being restored, and the rage of the expedition against the cockneys a little mollified by the steam it had let off, Mr. Philips plunged epic-wise into the middle of things.

"If I were called upon, gentlemen, to say what was the great especial characteristic of our American mountains, I would reply at once, their immensity—not the immensity of size, but of extent—that they fill the mind with the same order of sublime emotion that the ocean does, with this difference, that the sublimity, though alike in kind, is higher in degree."

"Good, good!"

"How clear he is!"

"The mountain sea is the actual sea enlarged to giant proportions. Standing here as we do now, and gazing out into the blue waves flowing in toward us from the distant horizon, I want to know, gentlemen, what sort of a ship would that be, to which these waves would rise mast-high?"

"What sort indeed?"

"Yes, you may well ask what sort! not such, I take it, as sailed of old out of Tarsus and Tyre, calling forth the deep wonder of Solomon; not such as swept the seas under Nelson at Trafalgar or the Nile; not such, even, as those that now sail under the star-spangled banner—that heaven-symbolized ensign—challenging the wonder of all mankind; not even leviathan, gentlemen, now in dock at Portsmouth—the Pennsylvania. Noah's ark, when it rode the highest wave of the deluge—the merest cockle-shell as it must have seemed in those mighty waters, would be a merer cockle-shell in these."

"Fine. How figurative is his style!"

"Like Jeremy Taylor's!"

"Something of the massive grandeur of Bishop Hooker's!"

"And the *perfervidum* of Milton's, with a discriminating infusion of the swash-buckler."

"And yet, gentlemen," continued Mr. Philips, knitting his brows, and concentrating his eyes to a focus, as if the object of all his bile stood before him, "and yet, though of such grandeur are these mountains, filling the mind with such nobility of thought, what means all this disparagement that is sputtered forth against them by the whole herd of modern travellers, abroad and at home, with some few honorable exceptions, who talk such downright arrant nonsense about them?"

"How effectually he puts a question!"

"What a fool-killer he would make!"

"The old Silenus riding an ass! Lambaste him well, Guy, while you're on him!"

"It is the burden of all these cockneys, gentlemen, and particularly of the John Bull, our cousin-germain, that our mountains are poor concerns. Why? Because (say these gentlemen fresh from the land of Cockaigne and thereabouts) when you have labored and toiled for half a day to get to the top of the highest Ararat or Taurus you can find, you can see nothing but endless mountains before you, and always in the farthest distant some giant higher still than that whereon, half-dead in climbing it, you foolishly expected to behold both the Atlantic and Pacific oceans."

"How he accumulates it upon them!"

"Piles the agony!"

"Wood up, County!"

"Throw in the bacon sides!"

"And not true this, even in fact, but miserably untrue. Why, look around you here as you stand. The refutation of the foolish nonsense is before your eyes. What are all these valleys, great and small—what all these dells and gorges, chasms, defiles, passes—these streams and rivers, rivulets and rills. Look at that drove of fatted beeves, winding yonder over the Knobley—the long column seemingly interminable. What have you to say to that lordly city of the far mountain plain, with all its towers and domes—its vast palaces looming up to the eye, and looming larger as you concentrate your gaze; visible only, it is true, to the imagination, acted upon through the deceived sense, but yet a nobler city than was ever built by hands!"

"Hold on, Prior, let's hear that again!"

"Don't speak, Trip; he's about to touch on something profound."

"And if such seeming cities, gentlemen, naturally arise to the eye here in the mountains—naturally, because the result of natural causes, what though in absolute fact there is no city there—what if it is illusion—all in my eye, as the vulgar say? It is only the reasoning mind that tells you this. The imaginative mind tells you there is a city: one part of your intellectual organization says there is not, another part tells you there is, and which do you believe? Most undoubted, as far as the present picture is concerned, the one that tells your sense that there before you stands the city. And there, to all intents and purposes, it does stand apparent before you, in all its magnified glory, such as was never built by human hands, such as can only be built by human brains, and those of the nobler order; a city up to the standard of the new Jerusalem, if your imagination is of the order of St. John's."

"Don't go in any deeper, Prior, or the subject will swim you."

"Devil the bit, it's good wading all about where he is."

"All this repeated cant, therefore, about our American mountains is not true in point of fact. But what if it were?—yes, gentlemen, what if it were? And this question brings me to the gist of the matter. According to the very statement of the cockneys, upon their own showing, the view now before them, is one that fills the human mind with ideas of the highest sublimity; for what, to the man of the largest comprehension, can be more impressively vast than this same immensity of mountain ocean that everywhere presents itself to view, with all its heaving, interminable, giant waves!"

"There you have knocked the swords out of the hands of the puny whipsters!"

"Killed them dead!"

"Dead as Julius Caesar!"

"It's a slaughter of the innocents!"

"It reminds me of the setting down Ulysses gave Thersites in the Grecian camp!"

"It's great spouting!"

"A whale's!"

"Swamping the pigmies in a deluge of ocean brine!"

"What senator he would make! how they would crowd the capitol when he let himself out!"

"He's rather high-strung, I think, for the modern democracy!"

"Not so, gentlemen, the very style and manner of eloquence—translucent, bold, free, combining imagination with reason—that has prevailed with all who speak the English tongue, from the days of Alfred the Great to the present time."

"Gentlemen of the expedition," resumed Mr. Philips, wiping the beads from his forehead, and with a self-sufficient air that would have done for the prince of Tyre, or Xerxes when he ordered the sea to be chained, "I think we have sufficiently *explained* the cockneys."

"Explunctified 'em!"

"All to smashes, Prior!"

"At all events, gentlemen, I've said my say—I've spit my spite, and my soul is now tranquil. With a serene exaltation I can again gaze over these *mountain billows*. The scene is indeed sublime! I hear "the mighty waters rolling evermore"—a sound as of the *poluphloisboio thalasses* is in my ear. What a manifold ocean! Here on the right is the classic

Mediterranean:—yonder monstrous promontory in among those jagged mountains is Scylla; and wo unto the mariner, who, eager to avoid its dangers, falls into the neighboring Charybdis's awful vortex! What a going round and round and round would be his! and what a swallowing up as he takes the suck—down—down—derry down, to the roaring music of the maelstrom. Oh! gentlemen, but it would be grand ship-wreck over there. Here to the left, where the shining valley shows itself, is the sunny Archipelago and the Grecian isles; and that grand city looming up from the waters is Athens—or you may have it old Troy—or the glittering city of Constantine, by the Thracian Bosphorus. There to the north are those 'uncouth, boisterous seas,' to whose mercy Francis Drake 'let go' all that was left of the *invincible* armada. Here's the Horn, and there's the cape 'of storms'—where you see the clouds gather. Yonder hazy point is Hatteras, and that tall naked pine is the mast of some yankee coaster, wrecked upon its fatal sands. All before me is the Atlantic; and down yonder, fast-founded by the wide-watered shore, some fifty sea-leagues hence, methinks I behold the lordly dome of our capitol, its gorgeous ensign peacefully flapping its folds over the land of the free and the home of the brave! And yet the cockneys say these a'n't mountains!"

"God bless the star-spangled banner!"

"And d—d for ever the cockney or what not, that would disparage, in any manner, the country over which it waves."

"At another time, gentlemen," observed the Signor Andante, "I could desire to add something to the glorification of our mountains, which the Prior hasn't condescended to touch upon:—it is in regard to the sylvan majesty of their scenery, in which they differ entirely from the European. You have no idea how bare the mountains abroad appear to our eyes, accustomed to these grand forests. In connection with this part of the subject, I would like to take the cockneys a turn or two, upon the splendor of the foliage in October—the hues of all dyes—particularly the scarlet—

> "' The leaves that with one scarlet gleam,
>   Cover a hundred leagues and seem
>   To set the hills on fire.'

"But we can't stay here all day." And the signor, without a word more, and with all that directness and determination of manner that characterized him, betook himself to his rheda—all the rest following—the Prior a little whetted by the exercise he took against the subjects of the king of Cockaigne.

CHAPTER V.

WINSTON AND ITS CASTELLAN—
MR. EDWARD TOWERS.

THE sun by this time is riding nearly midway in the skies, and we hasten on to the summit of the mountain, seven miles up from its base. We have climbed "the mightly Helvelyn;" and, what is more, we have said our say in doing it, to the honor and glory of the land, and the confounding of its enemies, their aiders and abettors. Here you gaze over the plateau of the wide Allegany ranges—some twenty miles across by the road; and far in the distance you behold the Backbone—the Taurus of the belt—down whose rugged sides the waters flow east and west into the far seas.

Some four or five miles on our way, more or less descending, on the side of a long hill that slopes down to Stony river, we stopped for the middle of the day at a large stone inn, kept open to the world by William Poole—Bill Poole seems to be his better-established designation hereabouts—from which familiar and easy manner of indicating him and his, we take

it he is a good fellow, a *bon camerado*, in his neighborhood. Mr. Poole was not at home, but he had left
a big viceroy over his dominions, under who lazy sway
some broiling and frying was accomplished, that
stayed a little that *sacred rage* about which we spoke
in the beginning of this chronicle. The hostler also
was absent; and finding no representative of that
very important official, we turned in and groomed
our own horses; and it was well done—which says
something as to the value of being able to take care
of yourself in this wide world. We took our coats off,
rolled up our sleeves, and "pitched in" to the work,
according to the formula prescribed in the stables of
Colonel Johnson, of Chesterfield—now dead and
gone—whose word was once law in all matters of
hippology—*horse-talk* the unlearned do call it.

"That hardihood," observed Mr. Butcut, as he
twisted a fresh wisp of straw, "which scales mountains, penetrates the wilderness, or subjugates the
beasts of the chase, while at the same time it re-
fuses to exert itself upon the needful well-being of
your horse, is but little to be commended."

"Right, Doctor Johnson!"

"The great Cyrus," said Doctor Blandy, "did not
think it beneath him to exercise his care over the
elephants he took with him on his expeditions."

"In Egypt, Napoleon always took special care of
the asses when he went into battle," said
Triptolemus.

"King Richard II., Shakspeare tells us, fed roan

Barbary with his own hands," put in the Prior, taking a long breath.

"If I am not mistaken," said the artist, "I have read it in the Iliad that Andromache herself fed Hector's horses—"

"To be sure she did!" said Trip, "and with grain which she steeped in wine."

"What is more directly to the point?" observed Blandy. "Let me remind you, gentlemen, of the personal care bestowed by Dugald Dalgetty upon Gustavus."

"Enough," said Mr. Butcut. "That man is little to be envied who does not feel himself all in a glow at having accomplished the generous labor of rubbing down his own horse. To my mind, it is an evidence of a princely disposition. Nothing, indeed, can be more honorable—when you can get nobody else to do it for you—but if I rub my 'Gustavus' again, if he never gets a rubbing, I hope I may never reach Winston!"—And Peter threw down his wisp, and washed himself in the horse-bucket, after the manner of a hostler.

With such like stable-talk—of which the above is but a small sample—we finished the rites, and left our Gustavuses to the enjoyment of their oats.

In due course of time we once more encountered the road; and after a drive of some twelve miles, over the undulating tops of this wide belt of mountains, down their gorges, through the passes, by farms lately cleared and green with wild timothy, bluegrass, and white clover—the natural growth of these fine grazing regions—we at length crossed the Potomac, and, winding up a long, fair sweep of hill, slackened rein before the gates of Winston.

It was somewhere about five o'clock when we won the stone, having driven some forty-three miles since we left the pleasant town of Romney in the early morning: forty-three miles of such delightful travel as can hardly be found elsewhere within our borders.

We hailed our resting-place with divers and manifold exclamations of surprise and delight, which brought the alert Towers to the hostel-gates, in a very broad-brimmed straw hat, stuck all over with fishing hooks and lines. The castle of Winston stands, like the castle of Richmond, "fair on the hill;" and although it did not greet our eyes with the feudal grandeur of Norham—with warders on the turrets, donjon-keep, loophole grates where captives weep, and the banner of St. George flapping idly in the breeze, as that famous hold met the gaze of Marmion and his train as they came "pricking o'er the hill," yet it looked cheerful and pleasant enough—had an air of something even like elegance as the western sun shed its splendor upon it. The porches with which it was arrayed imparted a look as of something "bedecked, ornate, and gay," like Delilah, Samson's wife, "this way sailing." Above all, it filled the mind perforce with comfortable thoughts of the mountain-breeze, as it spread itself out on the brow of a commanding hill—a grand hill, that stretches down for half a mile in bold, lawn-like sweeps, to the Potomac: the river here flowing along in all wild beauty, some twelve or fifteen miles below where it emerges, a wimpling rill, from the slopes of the Backbone.

The castellan or governor of Winston, Edward Towers, Esq., met us at the portals, with evident gladness in his heart. Right away, he called for his right-hand man Andrew, and proclaimed loud and quick his edicts in regard to horses, carriages, luggage, everything; every here and there something escaping his tongue, imprecatory of his or Andrew's eyes, or other parts of their bodies, such as their lights or livers, and even their diviner parts: his movements all the while in just keeping with his utterance, being wiry and terrier-like, up and down instead of longwise—energetic, sudden—just such action as hooks a trout without fail, and accounts for the governor of Winston's great reputation in these parts as a fisherman.

"Walk in, gentlemen," said, Mr. Towers; "walk in, walk in. Aha! well, indeed, you are here at last! Looked for you all day yesterday. Devil take me! Where did you come from to-day, gentlemen?"

"From Romney."

"By this time! Where did you dine—not at Reese's? Perhaps you had something with you?"

"We stopped back here some twelve miles, at a large stone house on the side of a hill."

"At Poole's—Bill Poole's. He went up above here to-day, fishing, d—n his eyes!"

"How are the trout, Towers?"

"There's nothing else in the water! I just took Andrew yesterday evening, and went up to the falls of the Potomac—slept out all night on the hemlock—and by breakfast-time this morning got home with over two hundred! How many, Andrew?"

"You're right."

"Yes, two or three hundred. Devil take me, if I couldn't have caught a three-bushel bag full as easy as not!"

This information was somewhat exciting, and gave rise to a desire, on the part of the more impressible members of the invasion, to commence demonstrations against the enemy forthwith. With this view, Doctor Blandy inquired of Towers the distance to the falls.

"About eight miles," answered the castellan quietly.

"And how is the road?"

"The road—road, did you say! The middle of the river is the best road I know."

"You can't ride to them, then?"

"There is a sort of a way over the hills, if you could find it. But that stops at the laurel, just before you come to Laurel run."

"What's the laurel?" asked Triptolemus, opening his eyes.

"You'll learn enough about it, Mr. Todd, before you leave here—more than you'll care about knowing, I reckon," observed Mr. Towers, with a smile of superiority at Murad's ignorance of the laurel. "The laurel, Mr. Todd, is the big laurel of these regions, that borders all the streams; and it's about as much as a man can do to get through it, let alone a horse."

"Ugh—uh!" replied Trip—which was a queer sort of laughing chuckle that characterized that gentleman upon all occasions.

It was clear that the falls of the Potomac were out of the question that evening; and notwithstanding all manner of trout were leaping up and down them in our mind's eye, we desisted for the present from any further investigations as to the way by which they were to be reached.

"But, Towers," said Mr. Botecote, authoritatively, "there must certainly be some place near here where we could have some pretty fair sport for an hour or so. I would like to add a few fish to your supper."

At this announcement, Mr. Towers looked a little astonished, and replied, confusedly—for Peter's manner was something lofty and imposing—

"Oh yes, certainly, Mr.— I really didn't hear your name—"

"Botecote," said Peter.

"Certainly, Mr. Botecote—I didn't think of that; I really thought now a couple of hundred might do you!"

"You started with two hundred, raised immediately to three hundred—may have four hundred by this time—and with all, Mr. Towers, I may possibly go to bed only tantalized with them."

"If there is one in the house this minute, there's four hundred, big and little! May the—"

"Be it so, then, Mr. Towers, and don't swear. I'll lay me down here on this settle, and methinks I'll take a nap."

"To-morrow, then, we'll begin the attack."

"Bright and early."

"When the hunter's horn is first heard on the golden hills."

"And I'll go with you," said Mr. Towers, "and show you the ground. We'll make a day of it—fish up to the falls and back. Those that don't want to go so far, can stay below here at some pools in the river. There's one pool that I call Ashmun's pool, after Mr. Ashmun of Massachusetts. May be some of you know him. Devil take my lights now, if he didn't pull out of that pool a basketful! One of them weighed a pound and a half; if it didn't, you may drown me!"

"Ugh—uh!" exclaimed Triptolemus.

"No doubt about it," resumed Towers. "You see he fished with the fly, which is a sort of curiosity to our fish, and rather takes 'em in for a little while. But give me the worm, after all."

"You fish with the worm, then, Mr. Towers?"

"Yes—anything I can lay my hands on."

"Did you ever try the bug?"

"The bug? what's the bug?"

"The Prior there has one. You ought to see it! I venture to say that every large trout in the stream will make at it."

"What's it like?" asked Towers.

"Here's a likeness of it," replied the artist, taking out his pencil, and drawing a rather exaggerated caricature of it.

"Devil take me," exclaimed Mr. Towers, "if it won't scare the biggest trout that ever swam the Potomac! That thing! Why, what sort of a bug do you call it?"

"It's called the trout hum-bug," said Peter.

"Well, gentlemen, I had thought that may be I might some time or other try the fly, and see what I could do with it; but if ever you get me to attempt that thing, may the—But there's no use talking about it. Come along, Andrew, and get out some oats for the horses. The best oats you ever saw, gentlemen. Hustle, Andrew!—hustle along!"

And so away hurried the castellan, with Andrew after him—Towers going off with a vehement, perpendicular movement, like one of the old grass-hopper engines on the railroad, when under a great press of steam.

"I think the Prior's bug was too much for our host," observed the artist.

"He's a worm-fisher!" said Doctor Blandy disdainfully. "If I were you, Prior, when I got my bug out to-morrow, I wouldn't let him come on the same side of the river with me."

"What a remarkably high mover he is!" said Trip.

"If the governor of Winston's performance comes anywhere near the promise of his speech and movement, we shall fare well, both man and horse." And this fair promise was not broken to the sense—it was fairly kept. The oats were as fine as ever grew—heavy, polished, hard, plump, and golden; and Andrew was only too liberal in dispensing them to each whynnying and pawing horse. As for ourselves, Gil Blas and Scipio ate no such supper in their retreat at Lirias. Fifty fine trout, all beautifully embrowned, and like Até, hot from—the flames below, came and went, and came and went again; and so lightly did they sit upon our bosom's lord, that it seemed all illusion—the insubstantial and pageant supper of a dream—to divest the mind of which fallacy, nothing but the appropriate disposition of a series of venison-steaks could suffice. After some protracted effort, however, in this way, the illusion was finally driven out from the mind, and we were happy in the content of the succeeding hours—hours spent in dreamy silence, or in easy conversation upon subjects appertaining to the gentle philosophy of Epicurus. And so, without a disturbing thought, indolently reclining around, we whiled the time away.

Thus passing the first hours of the night, at length we went to bed; and while yet conscious of bliss, sleep mingled itself stealthily in with the visions of the mountains and the rivers that were passing in ever-changing procession over the brain: each vision growing more indistinct as the long procession swept on—until at length, with the splash of some leaping trout in your ear, and his bright colors gleaming in your eye, sound and sight were gone. Such is the sleep of those who travel high mountain-regions, or sail the salt seas in temperate climes. Such was at first the sleep of this expedition, light as the early mist on the river. But, by-and-by, its folds descended more heavily upon us—heavy as a cloud; and then it became musical—ravishing the ear of the night with a varied harmony, a concord in discord of flutes, and soft recorders, and horns—the loud bassoon, with every now and then a turn of the hurdy-gurdy, and sometimes the drone of the bagpipe. Rossini is said to have caught the idea of the song of the barber, in his great opera, from the braying of an ass. Had he heard this sleep, a far more wonderful strain would have streamed forth beneath the fingers of the immortal composer! No Lilliputian slumber shall this chronicle record it, if I can help it—but rather that such as swelled grandly forth upon the night air, nightly, throughout the Brobdignag realms!

CHAPTER VI.

THE BLACKWATER INVASION DETERMINED UPON.

━━◆━━

THE head-fountain of the Potomac rises high on the eastern side of the dividing Allegany ridge, not far below the cone of the mountain, and near the boundary-stone planted by Lord Fairfax to mark the farthest limit of that princely territory—embracing all the country lying between the waters of the Potomac and Rappahannock rivers—which he inherited as a grant from the British crown. The Potomac is formed, in its very beginnings, by the union of several smaller springs with this head-spring, as they descend the steeps of the mountain. The little rivulet, pursuing its course along the base of the Backbone, is gradually augmented by the springs that flow down in every direction through the ravines around, until it attains a breadth of some thirty feet at the small falls, about five miles below its source. Below the falls there are some eight or ten streams making into it: the Big Laurel, Little Laurel, Sand run, and Shields's run, on the Maryland side; the

Horseshoe, Buffalo run, the Dog's Hind-Leg, and some others, on the Virginia shore. This accession of little streams swells it into quite a sizeable mountain-river by the time it reaches opposite to Winston. It is here some sixty feet wide—a clear, fresh, wild stream, reflecting every pebble that lies in its bed—shaded by stately forests, and fringed with vines and flowers. Of course, it is filled with trout; and although it is a good deal fished by those who frequent here in the summer, yet it still continues to yield up its treasure in sufficient abundance for the constant supply of the table at Winston.

For two days we made unceasing war throughout this Potomac region, as far up as the falls. The first day we brought in over two hundred fish, some of them of fine size. The second day we took more, having invaded some of the larger tributary streams mentioned above. So it will be seen we had trout in abundance.

When the third day came round, there was a general desire expressed, when we assembled at the breakfast-table, to foray in some new country. We had invaded the Potomac in all reason—having in these two days pretty well gone over the ground hereabouts. The mind of desultory man is still as studious of change, and pleased with novelty, under our republican order of things, as it has been heretofore under the older polities of the world. Indeed, it is a characteristic of our American Saxon, exceeding that of all others of the Saxon, or any other combination. . . . But where to go?—that is the question. Mexico has been taken—and where shall we find a Cuba? Some proposed an incursion into the Glades, over about Snow creek, said to be unfrequented ground: one was for the Evergreen-glades, another for the Oak-glades; some for the lower Potomac—but there were rattlesnakes down the river, it was said, and that was a damper. In this variety of opinion, the indolent policy prevailed: and it was determined to pass the day *sub tegmine*—rambling over the hills, and in the enjoyment of an easy, lounging time of it about the porches of the inn.

Sitting on the long porch that fronts the river, enjoying the cool breeze that seems always to fan these hill-tops, some mention, among our other talk, happened to be made of "THE CANAAN," or wilderness-country, over on the head-waters of the Cheat. It so happened that one of our party had been told, many years ago, that this land of Canaan was as perfect a wilderness as our continent contained, although it was not many miles away from the Glades on one side, and the long settled parts of Hardy and Randolph counties on the other; a country where the wild beasts of the forest yet roamed as unmolested as they did when the Indians held possession of our borders; a howling wilderness of some twenty or thirty miles' compass, begirt on all sides by civilization, yet unexplored. This statement was brought to mind by the casual mention of the country as we sat talking upon the porch; and it led to much inquiry in regard to the wilderness. Our landlord, as soon as the subject was broached, entered largely into it, and dilated upon the wonders of the Canaan in very glowing terms. It was only a few years ago, he told us, that elk had been killed upon its boundaries, not far from the settlements, at a place called the Elk-lick. He said there were deer in great herds—so wild, that they were almost tame. "And, gentlemen," he continued, with great animation, "if you can only reach the falls of the Blackwater, you can take more trout in an hour than you ever took before in all your lives."

"Ugh—uh!" exclaimed Triptolemus, with his usual chuckle.

"You don't tell me so!" said Peter, with open eyes and mouth.

"If you say so," resumed Mr. Towers, "we'll go into the country—Andrew can take care of the house—and we'll have such fishing as was never heard of. But understand now, gentlemen, you've got to do a little of the roughest and hardest sort of walking and climbing. Then there's the laurel you must go through. And you mustn't mind sleeping on hemlock, and in the rain too—it's always raining over on the Bone."

This was only applying additional stimulus to the desire that had already taken possession of us, and at all risks we determined to go on the morrow, provided we could secure the aid of two well-known hunters of this region to lead us on our way. Accordingly, we despatched a messenger to the house of Joe Powell, who lived on the borders of the Winston property, with a request that he would get John Conway, another hunter, living some miles farther off, and come down in the evening to see us. These men came over during the day, and it was all arranged before they left us, that we would set off in the morning early for the Blackwater.

Everything being put in train for the expedition, we gathered together on the long porch toward night-fall, and passed the time in much further discourse upon the Canaan—commenting variously on the information we had gathered from Powell and Conway, who had been out as far as the smaller falls of the Blackwater, hunting deer in the winter-season, but had never been at the great falls of the stream—the existence of which they only inferred from the roar of water that filled the forest, when they were out there.

In order that the reader may the better enter into the spirit of our wilderness adventure, we will take the liberty of introducing him more familiarly to our party.

In a large arm-chair, spread out to the extent of his bulk, with his feet resting upon a bench, and leaning back against the railing of the porch, sat a gentleman—stout, ample, and muscular—with a handsome face, rosy with bloom, and a pleasant twinkle of the eye, that told of the mirthful character of his mind. Just now, though, his countenance was grave and thoughtful. Rattlesnakes seemed to have taken entire possession of him, ever since we had determined upon our march into the wilderness; and presently he put the following question to Mr. Towers, with great emphasis:—

"Do you think, Mr. Towers, that my big fishing-boots—that very big pair, with the red tops, hanging up against the wall—will save me against the bite of a rattler?"

"Oh, bless you, Mr. Butcut, there are none in these hills. If there were, I can assure you, sir—may I be hang-danged if I would live here a single day—not even to own Winston! A rattlesnake, sir, has never been seen higher up this way than some two miles below yonder, at the foot of that mountain—and then only one—and he had to clear out. It don't suit 'em up here. Seven miles off yonder, on the side of that mountain, there is a den of them—where there are a plenty—so thick, you can smell 'em. But they stay down in that region, and never come up this way."

"That's what Powell says; for I took him one side, and ask him particularly about them. I think I would go into a fit if I should happen to tread on one of the blasted reptiles!"

"Make yourself easy about them. I pledge you my honest word, there a'n't any up here. The country's too cool, or something or other, for them. The devil take me—but I believe if I was to see one of them, I would jump clean out of my skin! I'm mon-strously afraid of 'em—and I confess it. I don't mind a wild-cat—he'll run from you: nor a bear unless it's a she-bear, with cubs—and then look out, I tell you! But rattlesnakes and copper-heads my nerves, some-how, won't stand. If I might take the liberty—you seem to have a little dislike to them yourself."

"If you would put on a pair of thick cloth panta-loons, and draw on a big pair of boots outside—such as mine yonder, Towers—I should suppose you would be safe from a bite."

"I should hate to trust them any way; rather not be struck at by them at all. Why, they have fangs an inch long!"

"What would you do, if one was to bite you?"

"Just lie down and die—give it up at once."

"Not so," broke in the artist; "no necessity for dying at all. Take out your knife, and cut out the flesh round where you're struck—suck the wound—then burn some gunpowder into it—and you're safe enough."

"Drink a pint or so of raw whiskey or brandy right off," observed the doctor, "and there's no danger."

"Not so much from the snake, may be."

"If I am not mistaken, I read an account, a year or so ago, of an experiment made before the French physicians, by which it was ascertained that a flask of olive-oil was a certain cure of the bite. Two coun-try-people came in, received the bite of a viper, swal-lowed a flask of oil each, and experienced no other harm than a little drowsiness for a few days."

"Swallow a good deal of sweet milk," said a coun-tryman sitting by. "I've known that to cure a man."

"Eau-de-luce," replied the doctor, "rubbed on outwardly, and taken internally to prevent coagulation of the blood, would be good."

"Well, now," said the countryman who spoke before, "for my part, I'm more afraid of a copper-head than I am of a rattlesnake; for he never gives you any warning. He's a night snake, too—he'll bite at night, and the other won't."

"How much olive-oil have you in the house?" inquired Peter.

"I don't believe there's any," replied Towers; "but I've got a plenty of castor-oil, if that would do."

"Have you any fish-oil?" asked Triptolemus.

"I think we had better drive a cow along," said Andante.

"What would you milk her in?"

"In the frying-pan."

"I am free to say, gentlemen," observed Mr. Butcut, "that I have more confidence in the brandy than anything else; and, as that is more at hand, we'll each take a flask with us, in case of accidents."

This proposition was readily assented to—and with it the subject of the rattlesnakes was about to be dismissed; but in the meantime the artist had taken out his pencil, and drawn a caricature of Butcut pursued by a rattler—his hair on end—eyes wide—nostril distended—fishing-rod, with a big trout on the end of it, dropped—and the rattler, with about twenty rattles on his tail, and his crest raised ready to strike, in hot pursuit! The caricature was well enough. The

castellan was both astonished and delighted. "Isn't it like him?" he exclaimed, and broke out into what an old-countryman of my acquaintance used to call an *imbrumpt laugh*, and took the drawing off to show it to his wife. Returning, he looked upon the Signor with more of deference than he had been disposed to show him before. His countenance had something of mingled wonder and delight as he fixed his eyes on him—some such expression as a man of the middle ages might be supposed to wear on his face as he gazed upon some imposing magician or sorcerer that had just performed a wonderful feat of art.

The rattlesnake terror had now altogether vanished. The caricature had killed it effectually; and the conversation took another turn.

"Towers, what wild animals are there over in the wilderness?"

"Plenty of them—bears, wolves, panthers, deer in crowds—some few elk, I reckon—and otters, and badgers—all the animals that ever were there."

"Do they ever attack you?"

"Not unless they are particularly hungry, which can't be at this time of the year. Your fire at night will keep them away from you, any how; though I have heard it said the panther has been known to walk between a party sleeping and the fire at their feet."

"That, I suspect, was a dream of some one who had gone to sleep with the wild beasts running in his brains."

"You have nothing to fear from the animals. The only thing you have to fear is losing yourselves. But Powell and Conway are good woodsmen; and, besides, they have been partly in the country. There is a story about, which I've heard ever since I've been living up here, that a good many years ago a stranger went into the Canaan, and was never heard of afterward. Years after, the skeleton of a man was found by some of the hunters that had ventured furthest into the country."

"That's very pleasant information for us, Mr. Towers. Do you think there is any chance of our leaving our bones out there?"

"Every man runs his chance."

"The devil he does! Why, this Canaan is not altogether more than some twenty or thirty miles of country in length, and, I suppose, not wider. How could a man well get lost in that compass?"

"Oh, very easily. Why, in those mountains a man could walk about for a week, from sunrise till sunset, particularly if he got into a big laurel-brake, and never at any time be five miles from where he started, unless he blazed his way."

Mr. Botecote mused somewhat seriously for a while upon this information, but finally came to the conclusion that the lost man and the skeleton was a fable, and that it was nonsense to talk about his being lost in any five miles of country. This seemed to be the conclusion of the rest of us. There is some such legend always told by the borderers upon every wild country. But, again, such things are rather probable. Men have been lost before in countries fare less wild than the Canaan turned out to be. However, we entertained no apprehensions of encountering anything worse than some endurable fatigue and hardship; and the conversation passed off into general pleasantry and merriment, in which the castellan of Winston came in for a pretty good share of rather free raillery, aimed at those more prominent peculiarities, which the reader will by this time recognise as belonging to him.

Murad the Unlucky, who had not said a word for an hour, but sat with his lame appurtenance thrown over the back of a chair, apparently drinking in the conversation like mothers' milk, now broke speech to the following effect:—

"Well, Mr. Powers, I've just been thinking what a mighty talker you are; you talk about like a horse I have at home runs. He beats everything in the whole country—but you can't rely on him; he won't keep the track."

"Why, you don't think so, indeed! Devil take my lights, I thought I was slow!"

"Don't you think you stretch it a little, Conners?" said Murad, expressing himself a little plainer.

"Every word true, Mr. Todd; blast my eyes! and more too; I haven't told you anything."

"What! all that about the rattlesnakes, and the bears, and the panthers, and elk, and such crowds of deer, and especially that about finding the bones of the lost man! Ugh! Uh!" Here Murad mused a moment, and went on. "Towels, are you any relation to the Conners down our way?"

It must be observed that Murad, among his other unlucky traits, had an unlucky way of confounding the names of all persons he encountered—a vice of his intellectual composition that nothing could eradicate; and so upon this occasion, Towers's name was mixed up in his mind with Powell's and Conway's— the two hunters—so inextricably, that he had none of them straight.

"To the Conners, did you say, Mr. Todd? The Conners! Devil take me, if I ever heard of any such people!"

"Why, as you are of the same name, I thought you might be some kin."

"May the devil!—blamenation!—if ever I saw— Conners—my name isn't Conners!"

"There you are, Trip—at it again," said Peter, who seemed to take Murad under his especial supervision. "I'll swear, gentlemen, he hasn't called any single man, woman, child, or horse—anything by a right name, since we left home. Why, Triptolemus, Towers's name isn't Towels, or Powels, or Conners, or anything of the sort. It's *Towers, Towers, Towers* —T-o-w, Tow—e-r-s, ers—Towers!"

"Well, what's the odds?" said Murad. "It don't make any such mighty difference. But you're some kin, a'n't you, Powels?"

"Well, I dare say I am, if I only knew distinctly which of my relations you mean. But what makes you think so?"

"Why, you talk so fast, and so much, that you remind me of one Connel, a lawyer down our way— a great pleader—who can out-talk any man I ever heard, until I had the pleasure of making your acquaintance; has a great gift of what they call the gab. You're a Virginian anyhow, a'n't you, Towels?"

"I don't know what he is now, but his ancestors came out of Babbleon," said the artist.

"Suffered under the old Babbleonish captivity," chimed in Galen.

"From which the race haven't yet been entirely redeemed," put in the Master.

"Well, that's pretty well; but, may the devil take me, if I don't think some of Mr. Todd's ancestors must have come out of the tower of Babel!"

"Right," said Peter—"right, governor. It's the only way of accounting for his confusion of names. And by the way, Trip, if you would bear the tower of Babel in mind, it might help you to get Towers's name right."

"It won't do," said the artist. "His mind is essentially a transposing one. He'd have it the bower of Table!"

"I give it up, then," said Peter, and he threw himself back in his arm-chair, with an air of resignation.

"Well, but, gentlemen," said the doctor, in his very pleasant, gentlemanly manner—(Galen was very deliberate when about anything like a witticism, and having studied one out to suit himself, some time back, he was determined that it should not be lost, notwithstanding the conversation that made it appropriate had gotten away from him)—"Well, but, gentlemen," said he blandly, and with a certain tickling sensation of pleasure upon his countenance, "this is letting Mr. Towers escape us. When we were running him about Babbleon just now, and fixing upon him a Babbleonish extraction, it occurred to me there must have been also some of the old Greek blood in him."

"How do you make that out, doctor?" said Towers, smiling.

"Why, by tracing your descent, Towers, in part, from the very famous old lawgiver of Sparta, Lycurgus."

"How is that? Who was this Lycurgus?" said the castellan, evidently very much flattered at the idea of being descended from any man with a name that he didn't understand.

"He was an old Greek, Towers—a Lacedemonian," said the Prior, taking up the doctor's idea—"an old fellow named Curgus, one of the Curguses of Sparta—a very remarkable family of people. But in the course of his life this old gentleman had told so many stories, about one thing or another, that by way of distinguishing him from the other Curguses, the people of his parts used generally to call him Curgus, the story-teller or romancer. The length of this designation, however, being contrary to the genius of the Spartans, who were a people of few words; they shortened it by calling him Lie-Curgus, which after a while came to be his received name."

"There were a great many other distinguished Greeks who acquired their names in the same way," observed the artist, "there are the Liesanders."

"And Lysemachus—a condensation you perceive, of *Lies he makes us*."

"The Greek genius is characterized, from the earliest ages, by an aptitude for invention."

"What monstrous fabrications some of those are which Homer relates!"

"Don't talk about them," said Triptolemus, "my back stings me every time I think of them. The whippings that I've had on account of them, are really horrible to think of."

"What were you whipped for, Mr. Todd?"

"Ignorance of Homer, Mr. Towels; undoubted ignorance, sir—clear—clear as day—not the least mistake about it. But my ignorance of that difficult language, Mr. Connel, was owing to my aversion to stories. Had Homer told the truth about the siege of Troy, I should have mastered him. You see, Towels, my feelings somehow or other were born on the Trojan side; and as soon as I began Homer I knew it was all a Greek lie: you may say, therefore, that I fell at Homer. But don't distress yourself at this little passage in my biography; I can assure you I haven't the same strong feelings in regard to your interesting account of the Canaan, although I must say I don't exactly believe all you tell us."

"May the devil roast my lights and livers, gentlemen, if I don't begin to believe you really think I have been stretching it a little about the Blackwater. Now do you know I haven't told you half I could tell you. The man's bones were found out there—I saw 'em myself—and for the deer, they are just in thousands; and as for bears, why one of 'em had Andrew by the throat—I mean, devil take my lights—up a tree down here for an hour, one day, not two miles from this house—yes, on Winston—and he shot him too—didn't you Andrew? And if you find a rattlesnake out there, why, I'll just give you leave to eat me, lights and all. As for the elk, I'll bring you a man, living not far from here, who will swear to you that he saw one himself, that was shot, not more than three years ago. Now I'll tell you what, gentlemen, I'll take an even bet with any of you, that you get lost notwithstanding you've got Powell and Conway with you—two as good woodmen as ever went into the woods."

"I don't care if we do," said the artist, "I'll fish in the Blackwater in spite of my bones."

"If all the wild beasts of the wilderness howl around my path, I'll stand by the Signor's bones," said the Prior.

"If I could only feel certain about the rattlesnakes," said Peter, "it would take off the only weight on my mind. But between my boots and the brandy, I will defy them."

"The idea of driving a cow in for the milk cure is abandoned, I suppose."

"Put up a plenty of provisions, Towers. I can stand anything better than starvation."

"Yes, gentlemen, and if you don't come back on the day you say, I'll get up a party and go in after you."

"Right—right; but I thought you were to go along, Mr. Powway."

"There you are again, Trip, it's intolerable—absolutely ridiculous. Will you never learn to call him Towers! You have no idea how it disturbs the flow of the conversation."

"I think, gentlemen," said Galen, delicately suggesting it, "that if Triptolemus would commit some verses to memory that had the word *towers* in them, he might possibly control this bias he labors under."

"A good idea—try it, Trip."

"Ugh—uh!" said Murad, with his peculiar ejaculation. "There you're too much for me again, I don't think I ever knew any in my life."

"Well, then, gentlemen, we'll give him some."

"Begin—some one."

"I will, willingly," said Peter.

"'Day sat on Norham's castled towers,'"—

"Day didn't," said the artist, "it set on Norham's 'castled *steep*'—that won't do. Try it again."

"I have a glimmering of a line that ends with *hostile towers*—but I can't make it out exactly."

"The gentle Surrey," said Galen, and then stopped short.

"What of Surrey?"

"I thought it was something about *towers*—but it isn't—it's 'loved his lyre.'"

"That's it—that will do," said Trip, "that will remind me of him—if you can find nothing better."

"There's a verse, gentlemen," said the Prior, "that has something about *towers bedight*—but I can't come at it. It ends with *temples and towers bedight*. Do any of you remember it?"

"Towers bedight!—Towers be d——d!—Lets go to supper," said the artist. And to supper we went—Towers bedight or Towers be-what you please, leading the way, and altogether delighted at the prominent figure he cut in the evening's conversation.

The supper had a subduing effect upon the vivacity of our spirits; and so, with a due regard to the Blackwater invasion on the morrow, we retired early to bed. The bright clear moon looked in auspicious through the curtains of our windows—and to the gentle lullaby of the Allegany night-breeze we fell fast asleep.

CHAPTER VII.

THE DALE ON THE POTOMAC—AND A SOMEWHAT PARTICULAR DESCRIPTION OF THE ARRAY.

⋅⋅⋅►◄✦►◄⋅⋅

I⊤ was somewhere about four o'clock next morning when we began to give out in sleeping; and so, lightly and airily, with gentle breathings, whisperingly, we now soon finished off the last delicate touches and roundings of our dreams about bears, and panthers, and rattlesnakes, and lost babes in the woods (meaning thereby ourselves), &c., &c., just as the early cock uplifted his clear clarion, and roused his dame Pertelotte and all the attendant damsels of the roost from their slumbers.

How finely our old first poet—he who

> "left half told
> The story of Cambuscan bold,"

—famous Chaucer—head of the English poet peerage—has pictured the gallant chanticleer:

> "His comb was redder than the fine corall,
> Embattled as it were a castel wall;
> His bill was black, and as the jet it shone,

> Like azure were his legges and his tone,
> His nails were whiter than the lily flower,
> And like the burned gold was his colour."

And how, with the soul of eloquence and poetry he makes him discourse—hear again:

> "He knew by kind, and by none other lore,
> That it was prime, and crew with blisful steven,
> The soune, he said, is clomben up on heven,
> Twenty degrees and on, and more ywis;
> Madam Pertelotte, my worlde's blis,
> Herkeneth the blisful birddes how they sing,
> And see the fresh flowers how they spring;
> Ful is mine harte of revel and solas."

And again; what a lordly cozener is our chanticleer—what handsome flattery of his Dame—and with what pleasant humor he trifles with the sex.

> "But let us speak of mirthe, and stinte all this,
> Of o thing God has sent me large grace,
> For when I see the beauty of your face,
> Ye ben so scarlet red about your eyen,
> It maketh all my drede for to dien:
> For all so sicker as, *in principio*
> *Mulier est hominis in confusio,*
> (Madam, the sentence of this Latin is,
> Woman is man's joy and man's blis.)"

And then how like a prince—royal in his port, and gallant is he—very much after the model of Henry IV. of France, when in the midst of *his* dames.

"He loketh as it were a grim leoun,
  And on his toos he rometh up and down:
  Him deigned not to set his feet to ground:
  He chukketh when he hath a corn yfound,
  And to him rennen then his wives alle."

The reader is now aware, that some time since, the early cock had proclaimed the morning. In the beautiful verse of Chatterton—

"The feathered songster chanticleer,
  Had wound his bugle-horn,
  And told the early mountaineer
  The coming of the morn."

It is now broad day, and the ruddy streaks are beginning to glimmer in the east. Up rise we, then, one and all, and shout aloud, "For the Blackwater!" The doors and windows are thrown wide open, and the mountain atmosphere—three thousand feet here above the sea—is all about us; and if you have never tried it, O unblessed lowlander! you can have no idea of its extremely animating powers: there are few things more stirring to both body and soul. It compels to many extravagances of both speech and action. Especially it makes you sing, whether you can or not: and so it was that, chanting songs of the morning, we made our orisons to the god of day, Phoebus Apollo, now emerging in all-unutterable glory through the golden portals of the east:—

"Thou splendid luminary! honored, in some form or other, by all the nations of old; proclaimed prince of the lights of heaven throughout all the realms of Christendom; worshipped by the barbarian, wonder of the savage; saluted in thy rising with the clash of cymbals and gongs, and the flourish of trumpets and horns, the roll of drums, and the roar of morning guns; man everywhere doing thee homage—in the old East, prostrate with slavish adoration; here in the new West, standing erect (as I do now), and with dilated chest, pouring out his soul in hymns of praise, as befits his free-born nature!—Great God-send of all mankind! particularly of all poets and orators; filling the world with the grandest of the grandeurs of simile, and trope, and metaphor; also at the same time usefully beneficent in imparting both light and heat, without which this earth would be about as dark and cold as a rat-hole, and almost as fit to live in—really the dim spot that a disconsolate philosophy would make it out to be!—Beneficent and beautiful mystery! such as thou art here in thy rising over these broken and piled-up Alleganies; lighting up the grand countenance of Nature around, as with smile and the glory of a god! no wonder that all languages and tongues, even from the Chaldee down to our modernest Brother-Jonathan dialects, should be exhausted in the utterance of such a worship."— ("Good-morning, Mr. Towers. You seem to be in considerable astonishment. Take a seat. The expedition, through Mr. Butcut, is addressing the great luminary, whose gorgeous rising we take to be a happy omen for our enterprise.")—"Fountain of light and life!—hailed by the choir of birds; encircled by clouds of gold; fair as a bride and fiery as a bridegroom! *thee* to resemble—thee!—that was the very boy's first wish and and proud desire, through every vicissitude of fortune, amid the glitter of prosperity, above the tempests of mischance, to maintain an undecaying splendor!"

After this address to the rising Splendor—part of which was made once before by Alcibiades when a banished man in Thrace at the court of King Seuthes—where, it will be remembered by the learned reader, he outdrank the whole barbarian court—the king, queen, princes, courtiers, warriors, ladies-in-waiting, and all—thus fulfilling his matchless destiny—peerless in everything, even in these wild Thracian orgies—after this address to the great luminary, we speedily arrayed ourselves, and forthwith appeared below-stairs, as respectable and picturesque a set of outlaws in appearance as ever robbed a rich grandee of his gold, plundered monastery or cathedral of old of its molten gold and silver, or bore away shrieking maiden to the hidden fastness in the forest.

It was in this order that we began our march: Three of us were on horseback, with wallets hung across our saddles, containing the provant for the expedition—which provision consisted of six large loaves of bread; some pounds of ground coffee; sugar; about ten pounds of middling of bacon, to fry our trout with; a boiled ham; salt, pepper—and that's about all. Cigars and tobacco to smoke, each adventurer carried about his own person, together with a flask of spirits to cure himself in case he was bitten by a rattlesnake, or peradventure to prepare his system beforehand against any deleterious effects from the bite—a somewhat unnecessary precaution, indeed, since we were all pretty well convinced there were no snakes in the Canaan.

Three of us were afoot—two of our original party and Powell, one of the hunters—he equipped, among other things, with his rifle; Conway, the other hunter, we were to pick up on the way.

We were to ride and walk alternately—ride and tie—until we reached the end of the settlements, which was as far as we could take the horses.

Pursuing the Northwestern road some three miles, we reached the top of the Backbone ridge. Here, turning at right-angles to the left, we followed a mountain-road along the top of the ridge for some miles, which at length took its course along the eastern side of the mountain, gradually growing into a mere single horse-track, until we reached Conway's house, the last settlement in this direction. Here we picked up Conway, with his rifle and frying-pan; and after a walk of some six miles or more through a most noble forest of sugar-trees, the beech, maple, wild-cherry, balsam-firs, and hemlocks, and over tracts of land wonderfully fertile, judging by the great size of the trees, and the growth of the wild timothy upon one or two slight clearings we passed through,

we at length descended into a beautiful little glade
—more properly a dale in the mountains—some three
hundred yards wide and two or three miles long,
where we were to turn out our horses to pasture
until our return.

This dale is girt round upon its edges by a broad
belt of the *Rhododendron*—commonly called the *big
laurel* out here—which makes the dale a safe enclo-
sure for keeping our horses; for it is impossible that
a horse can make his way through it, so thick and
lapped together everywhere are its branches. We had
to enter it by a path cut out for the purpose. When
within, we barricaded the entrance by piling up some

young trees and brushwood (which was equivalent to putting up the bars in a fenced field), and rode on down the middle of the wild meadow, through green grass, knee-high, and waving gently in the summer wind, until we reached a small stream, whose banks were overgrown with osiers and other delicate shrubs. This was the infant Potomac, destined before it reached the sea to expand into that mighty river on whose broad bosom whole navies may ride in safety or "flame in battle;" and also famous all over Christendom for that it holds fast-founded by its shores the capital of the star-emblazoned republic. Here we halted and dismounted—took off saddles and bridles—turned our horses loose—and prepared ourselves to enter the untrodden wild that rose up before us, dark with the glimmer and the gloom of the immemorial woods!

Before the expedition moves, it is necessary that we should enter into a few particulars descriptive of the adventurers in the new aspect in which we are about to present them to the reader.

Behold, then, at about one o'clock in the day, the knights-errant of the Blackwater, in the middle of this little grassy dale of the Potomac. Let us point them out to the reader by name, and in a general way by character.

First, there stands before you a slight, elastic, and somewhat gaunt gentleman, with a dark, concentrated eye, sunk deep beneath a marked and rugged brow. The expression of his face at present is particularly indicative of that sort of energy and determination of character, which is very apt to make its possessor what is vulgarly called *head-devil* in all matters of feud, foray, or whatever enterprises that might be classed under the designation of marauding—all dare-devil achievements. The imagination of the wilderness before him, has called into play these latent qualities of his nature. This gentleman wears a beard, after the fashion of the middle ages, that has held undisturbed possession of his lower face for now some fifteen years; with all his present surroundings, it gives him the look of a brigand as in a picture; meet him in the streets of a capital, and it would impress you with the idea that he was a practitioner of astrology, or some other occult matter—may be some Italian philanthropist, or revolutionary conspirator—the friend of liberty all over the world, wherever liberty had a market: his disdain of a feather and all melo-dramatic show of appearance, precludes any idea of the Hungarian, as recently impressed upon our minds. He wears a green cloth cap, with a straight, projecting square visor to it, like the European military caps. An old black coat, with gray pantaloons, and a pair of rough boots with large red tops—these drawn on outside complete his dress. He has no small wallet strapped to his back—a blanket and a great coat rolled up constitute it. Around his neck is suspended an artist's sketch-book. In his right hand is a frying-pan. This is our artist, the Signor Andante Strozzi.

Of course, he is of the illustrious Florentine family of that name, some one of his ancestors having escaped from the feuds and broils of Italy, some centuries ago, and taken refuge on these shores. The name has changed so much in the course of time, and one thing and another, here with us, that you would hardly recognise it, as it is spelt and pronounced now in these days of democratic disdain of all things appertaining to a man's name and lineage. We, however, his more learned friends, and not too extreme in our democracy, choose to call him, according to the old Italian spelling and sound—Strozzi. There is a Dutch family in Pennsylvania, the Strodes, who are disposed to trace their origin in the same way from the Strozzi; but this they have no right to do. The Strodes are Teutonic in their descent; they are the old Saxon—the undoubted High Dutch: Stride was the name originally. The Strides, Striders, Strodes, and all these, are of German extraction, and in fact the same people originally. Our friend is the true Strozzi, however; and he shows his Italian origin by the peculiar beard he wears, his love of and genius for the arts (particularly those of painting and music), and some slight brigandish characteristics that belong to him, which last make him a somewhat dangerous antagonist for man or beast to dally with, and therefore one in every way the very person for an expedition into the Canaan—a man who would laugh a bear in the face, and take particular pleasure in pitching into a panther; one who would be about as careless of consequences in any encounter as either of these two last-named gentleman! So much for the Signor Andante Strozzi.

That stout, thick-set, well-knit gentleman, whose manner is somewhat eager, with face in a glow, eye red, and mouth open—look at him! He is laboring at present under an undue quantity of excitement. The idea of the wilderness has electrified his system into intense sensation. His ideas are exaggerated out of all bounds. He has just finished strapping on his shoulders an immense wallet, big enough for a mule to carry. But he looks stout, and broad, and strong—is well made—and you think it is all right, and that he has generously loaded himself according to his greater power. Well, he'll be tested presently. This is the gentleman who had the pleasant conversation with Towers yesterday, on the porch, about the rattle-snakes. He wears an old brown sack-coat. His boots are drawn on outside his pantaloons, and they are very big, and stout, and rough, and reach up to his knees: he bought them as a special defense against the rattlesnake. On his head he has a broad-brimmed, black, slouch hat. On his shoulders he has the aforesaid large roll. In his right hand he has a stick of laurel, with portions of the root attached, and which is as tall as himself. Tied to his waist behind is a bit of sheepskin with the wool on it, that he may have something soft to sit down upon when he rests himself in the wilderness. You perceive he goes in for the conveniences of life. On the whole survey of this gentleman, you would say that he was the make and look of a man to lift or carry a heavy weight, or to pull up a sapling by its roots—to hit a hard blow; good at knocking down and dragging out; but not the best show of a man for a hard walk, or climbing mountains, or getting well through a half-mile brake of the rhododendron. This is Mr. Butcut.

That thin, sinewy, hard, tough-looking gentleman, resting himself upon his sound leg, which is his left, and a-tiptoe on his right, which is his broken one, shortened and stiffened at the knee, is Mr. Triptolemus Todd—our Murad the Unlucky. In consideration of his lameness, it has been decreed that he shall carry no burden; yet of his own accord he has mounted Powell's rifle, the muzzle of which he has pointed right in among us; but, as he is undoubtedly the most heedless man in the United States, we have taken care that there shall be no priming in the pan. This remarkable gentleman's mind has been, somehow or other, impressed with an extraordinary idea of the wonderful and amazing in regard to the Fairfax stone, and he is now looking away off up the dale, as far as possible, to see if he can't discover it. He has a confused idea in his mind that this Fairfax stone is the biggest thing of its sort in the state of Virginia; but he has no definite idea about it: it may be like the rock of Gibraltar, or the rock of ages; it may be a basaltic pillar, like Lot's wife, or it may be a great, huge tablet, upon which some boundary hieroglyphics have been carved. Of course, therefore, he has no very definite idea of the sort of thing he's looking for. Just at this moment something vague looms up before his intent gaze into the distance, and his face is all ablaze with excitement as he exclaims, stretching his long, sinewy arm far before him, with his fingers spread out, and all pointing different ways—"*Fellows, yonder's Fairfax's stone!*" Murad is a light, wiry man, of some five feet ten inches in stature; and, without going into particulars, we will only say of him that he has a look of exposure about him, as if the heavens—cold and hot—the suns of August and the snows of December—had been contending for him for many years, with such equal success, that neither of them had been able to take him entirely. His dress is a very indifferent one. It is torn in several places already; and the fear is that before we get back he will have none of it, and that we shall have to paint him, or rather stain him with the juice of berries, to preserve him from absolute exposure—fix him up like Prince Vortigern—

> "A *painted vest* Prince Vortigern had on,
> Which from a naked Pict his sire had won!"

To tell the whole truth in regard to Murad, there never was a man that went upon an expedition of any sort with so little preparation and under such unlucky circumstances. He had but one suit of woollen clothes with him, all the rest being light summer

linens, of no use here. His pocket-book, with some
bank-notes in it, he left behind upon his table, and
had only a small purse with some six or seven dollars of silver in it. He had a note in bank for a thousand dollars, due three days after he left home, and
for which he had made no provision; and, in the hurry
of shaving himself to get off in time, he had cut a
great gash in his cheek, which gave him a look as of
a sabre-cut received years ago at some such battle
as Borodino or Waterloo, or on Pompey's side at
Pharsalia, where Caesar's veterans aimed at the
face.—But enough of Mr. Todd: the reader will now
be able to picture him sufficiently well for the purposes of this narrative.

The next gentleman that we shall introduce is
Doctor Adolphus Blandy. You see him there over on
the other side of this little rivulet, the Potomac, in
the act of taking an affectionate leave of that powerful dapple-gray with the bobbed tail. He has just
imprinted a kiss upon the soft muzzle of the gray.
His gentle heart is touched that Rinaldo has to be
committed to the rude mercy of the wild beasts of
Canaan for so many days; and with a tear of repen-
tance that he brought him here, and a sigh of regret
that he has to leave him, has made his farewells—
half in fear he shall never see Rinaldo again this side
of horse-heaven. The doctor is a very dainty gentleman, and given much to personal elegance of life.
He is equipped at all points. His large boots come
fully up to the knee, and they are soft and pliable,

made of the best French leather. His doublet-coat is substantial, with many convenient pockets, and fits him comfortably. He has a quarter-dollar rough straw-hat, tied round with a red riband in a good bow-knot. As he is near-sighted, he wears a pair of gold spectacles. Blandy is a large, fine-looking man, and he is of an easy and gracious presence. There is a sort of disdain about him of the big wallet that he has strapped to his shoulders; he seems to feel that it should be borne by a menial. He has evidently been trained to a life of luxurious ease—like Dives, has been clothed in purple and fine linen, and fed daily upon dainties. *Ennuied* with indulgence, he has come into the wilderness, to purchase, at the expense of its hardships, a new zest to his existence—a zest which the fortune of his condition can not otherwise afford him.—But enough of Blandy. Let us picture to you another gentleman,—remarkable among the sons of men—also among their daughters.

There, off at the edge of the vale, at the foot of a branching tree, stands one who is no bad idea of the famous knight of La Mancha, if you would only suppose the immortal Don to have been not quite so raw-boned as history has recorded him. This gentleman is somewhat tall, and of a loose and dangling aspect, in keeping with the somewhat careless ease of his character. To look at him now, as he stands, you would suppose him in the act of propitiating the god of the wilderness with votive offerings; for he has just finished hanging up on the lowermost branches of that beautiful and fairest tree all the saddles and bridles, and other horse-equipments, rowelled spurs and whip, &c.; and with his large and lustrous eye ("heaven-eyed creature," as Wordsworth calls Coleridge) resting in pleasure upon the picturesque grouping he has effected of them, you easily imagine him some deep enthusiast of the forest, hanging his votive offerings upon the wilderness-god's shrine. Lingering he stops, absorbed in what he has done; then turns slowly away, and having reached the party in the middle of the dale, he exclaims earnestly, "Well, gentlemen, I don't think the wild beasts can eat up our saddles and bridles, spurs and whips, any how—no matter what they may accomplish upon our horses!" This gentleman is Mr. Guy Phillips—the County Guy—the Prior—but more properly the Master of St. Philips, for St. Philips is the name of his hold, where he keeps the world at bay. He is somewhat tall and delicate of form, of a high visage and a lofty carriage—and, as we have said, taking away the idea of the gaunt appearance of Don Quixotte, is not very unlike that immortal champion of the right and redresser of the wrong. The Master is a man of middle life, and has seen something of both man and woman in his time, both high and low. In many a gay and glittering scene of revelry has he wasted the golden days of his exuberant youth—his heart swelling to the sounding minstrelsey, and his soul entranced by love and beauty. And also, like the good Lord Clifford, he has been

"In huts where poor men lie"—

and there learned a wiser lore than life could other-wise teach him. The Master has long since learned much sound knowledge in his time—that pleasure is of the things that perish in the using—that woman's looks teach but folly—that there is a great deal of good sense in the Proverbs of Solomon, and wisdom in the Ecclesiastes, &c., &c.; in fact, he has begun to know that Solomon was a very wise man: and, arriving at this distant glimpse of truth, he has taken to the woods and rills, and has learned how to be reasonably happy. But what would she, the beau-tiful Mary Dale, think of him could she see him now—he who erewhile basked in the sunshine of

"Her eyes' blue languish, and her golden hair!"—

could she see him now, his whole countenance shed-ding rays of joy in every direction, like a golden *au-reola* on an angel's brow, as he puts his hand to his mouth and sounds a loud and prolonged bugle-call from out the midst of this lovely dale, while all the mountains round cry out responsive with their thou-sand voices! "Alas, poor Guy!" she would say, "I little thought when surrounded by mirrors that multiplied our image, in rooms gorgeously festooned with hang-ings of burnished gold and silver, and reclining on couches softer than the bed of roses the emperor Verus dreamed himself away on—I little thought that you, then stealthily playing with the tangles of my hair, and openly fettered by my eye, would ever come to such wild destiny as this!"

The reader may now picture to himself our two guides, the hunters Powell and Conway, and he has the party complete—Powell a thin, sinewy, and yet muscular man, with long, straight locks falling down from his head like strands of rope; with a pillow-case thrown over his shoulders, in which was our provision: and Conway a short, wiry, stringy, thick-set little structure of whipcord, equipped in like manner as Powell—each with his rifle and pouch.

But we are dallying too long here in the dale— we must up and away! Let us begin the march, how-ever, in another chapter.

CHAPTER VIII.

THE MARCH INTO THE CANAAN.

P<small>OWELL</small> is in the lead followed by Conway, and we all start with a shout upon our walk—jumping the baby Potomac with a bound, and falling into a line of single file—winding through the long grass by a track made by the deer coming down into the dale to drink. The Signor waved his frying-pan aloft, and shouted out gayly the burden of some old hurrah song. The Master doubled up his hand and blew upon it for a buglet. Peter capered along nimbly, in dancing measure, like a fairy on the green—big wallet and all. Trip threw out his game leg, sweeping it against the tall grass, as a mower sweeps his scythe. And the Doctor took his last lingering look of Rinaldo—waved his lily hand and sighed adieu—

> —"Adieu, for evermore, my love,
> And adieu, for evermore!"

The horses snorted and plunged around us, with their tails flung over their backs, and hovered along our line, until we came to the belt of laurel that girts the edge of the meadow, when they wheeled, and left us to our fate—and we them to theirs. In a few moments we were breaking our way through the thick tangled branches of the laurel, and in mud and water half up to our knees. But we fought the way gallantly, and, gaining the firm ground, began the ascent of the mountain by a winding deer-track—the same we had followed through the dale.

About half a mile up we halted by the little Elk-lick—a deep and wood-embosomed *gouge*—as the hunters called it—in the side of the mountain, filled with black marsh-ooze, in which were little pools of stagnant, saltish water. Here the boldest held his breath for a while, in expectation of getting a shot at a deer. But whatever chance there might have been for this, it was soon destroyed by the loud outcries of Mr. Butcut, who was yet some distance down the mountain. Presently that gentleman came up, with his face about the color of a full-blown peony, the perspiration rolling down from him, and blowing hard like an over-driven horse. "Oh! I'll be—if I can stand this," he gasped out vehemently. "By the Apostle Paul! gentlemen"—(Peter is very familiar with Shakspeare, and is the best amateur actor of high tragedy in our country to-day; had he gone on the stage early in life, he would have undoubtedly acquired an unsurpassed name in our theatrical annals)—"By the Apostle Paul! gentlemen," he exclaimed in a manner unconsciously tragic, "this mountain has cast more terror into the soul of Richard than he can well endure." And relapsing immediately into the commonplace, he went on. "And don't you all know well enough, gentlemen, that I'm rather thick-winded at best, and here you have fairly run away from me up this infernal, all-fired hill, as you call it—hill indeed! Powell, how far are we from the top?"

"Not more than a mile or so, I reckon, Mr. Butcut."

"A mile or so! There it is—I knew it would be this way. Fellows, let's turn back." This he said bigly. It was received with a burst of derision. "Let me make a proposition. If you turn back I'll agree to pay all the expenses of the expedition, from home and back."

"Fiddle-de-de!" said one.

"Devil take you and all expenses of all sorts!" said another.

"Not for your whole estate, in fee simple!" said a third.

"No money can buy us!" said Triptolemus.

"Hear me, gentlemen," said Mr. Butcut, entreatingly, "of course I had no idea that the money could influence you. I didn't mean that. I'll give the money to any charity you may designate. And Powell and Conway, I'll give you five dollars more than you were to get."

"Not so!" said the artist, "you shall do no such thing!"

"We don't want anything more than was agreed upon!" said both Powell and Conway.

"Ugh, uh!" said Triptolemus. "You advised me not to come, did you!"

"You'll get along better, Peter, after the first blow or two!"

"The *acquirit vires eundo,* will apply to you after awhile, But, don't entertain any despair!"

"I can't stand it, gentlemen, I tell you, and carry this load on my back—I'm no horse!"

It will be perceived by the reader, that Mr. Butcut made a very determined attempt to break up the expedition, here at the Elk-lick, but all to no avail. His mutinous designs were promptly crushed in the bud. It being clear that nothing was to be gained in this way, he was determined that he would get rid of his burden.

"Well, gentlemen," he said, laughing, "I confess that I've failed in my vigorous effort to turn you back: that's no *go* certainly:—of course I wasn't in earnest. But really, seriously speaking, I'm no horse, and can't carry all this load."

"What's a blanket and a great-coat to a stout man like you, two feet and a half at least over the shoulders?"

"If you think it's nothing, suppose you just feel it." Here he unstrapped his wallet, and handed it round for inspection. It was, in fact, a great deal heavier than any of us had imagined, large as it looked. So it was determined that he must be lightened of his load. Accordingly the wallet was unrolled—and no wonder it was so heavy; for instead of containing merely a single blanket and a greatcoat, the blanket was found to be a large new double one, and in addition to this, there was an old, thickwadded coverlet of a bed, commonly called a Yankee-blanket, that had been used as a saddle-blanket, until it had grown doubly heavy from the grease and perspiration it had accumulated in a long horseback service. Peter, very provident of his creature comforts, with the intention of being extra luxurious when in camp at night, had very quietly, and unknown to the party, secured this treasure to his own use. It was really, therefore, no such great wonder that the first half-mile of the Backbone had been too much for him. Such a mountain is a pretty stiff encounter for a man of no superfluous flesh, and the soundest lungs—and so the lightest of us found it; but a thick-set, stout-built, two hundred pounder of a gentleman, yet in the soft condition, and with not the best breathing apparatus in the world—a butcut like But, will attest the quality of his metal, whenever he attempts to match himself against the Bone of the Alleganies, and that, too, even though he has not a heavy-wadded blanket additional in his wallet.

The reader will understand now, that the only thing really the matter with Mr. Botecote, was that he had overloaded himself, as was intimated when we were down in the dale of the Potomac. So, hanging the discountenanced encumbrance upon a limb of the nearest tree, he took heart again, and once more grew animated with all the hope of the Blackwater.

"Come, move on, men," he exclaimed, as he strapped on his shoulder his now diminished burden. "This is something like. I can stand it now with any of you. Move on, Powell."

And the expedition moved again. It was hard work in good earnest. But we went on up the rugged steep, scrambling our way as best we could, now through the thick underwood, now in among great masses of rock, and over fallen trees so decomposed that they would not bear your weight, until we reached what seemed to be the top of the mountain. Here those who were foremost called a halt, and sat down to rest upon a mossy log that imbedded you for about a foot. The others came straggling in— Triptolemus falling in, with his arms spread out before him, and his lame leg out in the air behind, as though it didn't belong to him, and crying out as he pitched in, "I say, fellows, is this Fairfax's stone? Ugh—uh! Here I am!"

"Fairfax's stone!" said Peter, getting it out as his breath would allow. "Fairfax wouldn't have climbed this hill for all the six millions and a half acres of his inheritance. I take it he was a man of too much sense.

Heavens—but I'm nearly gone! How far are we from the horses, Powell?"

"About two miles, I take it. It's about two miles, Conaway, up to here? Yes—so I thought."

"Come, move on, men. There must be no mutinous conversation indulged in. Peter's for a revolt again, I see," said the Signor.

Peter was now rested, and he resented the imputation with many valorous words.

"No, gentlemen, no such trifle as this wilderness shall prevent me from fishing in the Blackwater! It isn't more than two or three miles off, Powell, is it? And down hill, you say, from here?"

"We are over the worst of it now, Mr. Butcut," said Powell.

"Move on men—move on men," said Peter, "but don't go too fast—I'm afraid Mr. Todd can't keep up with us."

"Ugh—uh! Never mind me, I can get along with any of you." And here Trip pitched over a rock and disappeared (his game leg last) into a thicket, laughing out his *ugh—uh!* and presently he came into line again, as if nothing had occurred more than he looked for.

The wilderness was growing wilder. We had, some time since, lost all trace of anything like even a deer-path. Still, pleasantly, and in fine spirits, we pursued our way. Now we had to climb some steep hill-side, clinging to the undergrowth to pull ourselves up, and now we would come up against a barrier of fallen trees—some of them six feet high as they lay along the ground, and coated with moss half a foot thick—some so decomposed that they recreated themselves in the young hemlocks and firs that grew up out of them—some more recently fallen, with great mounds of earth and stone heaved up with their roots; these mounds sometimes covered over by other trees thrown across them, and thus affording shelter to the wild animals from the snows and storms of winter. Over all these we would climb and roll ourselves across; and sometimes, such obstruction did they present to our course, we would be obliged to make a detour round for the length of a quarter of a mile may be, and find ourselves only advanced a hundred paces on the straight line of our route. It was thus we went along—up-hill and down—now along the side of a rib of the mountain—now over its cone, and now along it—down through deep ravines and up out of them, and scarcely able at any time to see further ahead than some twenty yards, so thick were the leaves about us; and not often able to catch a glimpse of the sun, so dense was the mass of foliage *umbrellaed* out everywhere above us. Still there was a great wild delight in it all; and by this time we had become somewhat inured to the work; we were beginning to improve in condition, and we felt our sinews and muscles coming into better play every step we took.

After awhile, thus pursuing our steady advance, we came to a small rivulet, trickling its way down a shallow ravine, and evidently making its course to the west. This was a little rill that sent forth its mite, high up in these loftiest regions, to form the waters of the Cheat river; the Cheat falling into the Monongahela—the Monongahela into the Ohio—the Ohio into the Mississippi—and so to the great Atlantic reservoir. It was clear, now, that we were on the other side of the Backbone.

"This water, gentlemen," said Powell, "is making for the Blackwater. We are across the Bone."

"How far now, Powell, before we reach the falls?" asked Peter.

"Well, I reckon about four miles—maybe."

"Four miles! It can't be. It's no such thing. Why, Mr. Powell, didn't you say distinctly, that it was but four miles altogether from the place we left the horses."

"Oh, no—I didn't say that! I told you, we *could* bring the horses along to within about four miles of the falls—over to another glade, which we will come to before long."

"I'm deceived, gentlemen. We have all been deceived by these men. Conway is this the case that Powell says?"

"Powell knows the country better than I do. He's nearly right, I guess. I should suppose now, we are about four miles away."

"Gentlemen, hold on—stop," said Peter, "I've a proposition to make."

"You had better not be left behind," said the Signor, "you might get lost out here. Keep up with the line."

On we went, increasing our pace a little, for the day was hying westward; and if we intended to reach the Blackwater by nightfall, there was no time to waste.

"This is intolerable!" said Peter. "It's all non-sense—not a particle of sense it. I say—hold on, I've a proposition to make."

"I don't think we are treating him right," said the Doctor, a little tired himself. "It isn't fair—he might be suffering. We ought to halt, and hear what he has to say."

As Peter's voice was strong—altogether unimpaired, there was a rather general impression that there was a good deal of good walking in him yet. But we halted and threw ourselves down upon the moss.

"What's the proposition? Let's have it while we are resting—for there's no time to lose."

"Well, gentlemen, it strikes me we ought to encamp."

This was met with a general dissent.

"It's my opinion we are lost," continued Peter, "decidedly lost. These men have deceived us. They start out by telling us that it's only four miles from where we left our horses to the Blackwater. Well, we left them at one o'clock, and it's now five by my watch. We've been four hours in coming here—and I'm nearly dead at that! Now they tell us they've got yet more than four miles to go! I don't believe they know themselves where we are. I believe we are lost, and that we are walking about here for nothing. Powell, tell me, didn't you say just now that this little rivulet was one of the sources of the Blackwater?"

"Yes—and I think so still, Mr. Butcut."

"Only think so! There it is, gentlemen. He don't know where he is. I don't believe we are near the Blackwater."

"Nor I either," said Triptolemus, who grew uneasy at the idea of being lost—remembering the story of the lost man, and the bones that were found out here. "If I could have seen Fairfax's stone, I might have had some confidence. How can this little stream make the Blackwater, when it's as white and clear as any water we have seen?"

"Yes, Murad's got it! How can it be, Powell?"

"Well, gentlemen, it's no use talking. I am in the right direction. Don't you say so, Conaway?"

"Yes, I do."

"Well, that's all," continued Powell, a little miffed for the moment, "that I can do for you. There a'n't any finger boards out here to point out the way. All I can do for you is, to take a general direction right, and I know I must hit the Blackwater somewhere—a mile or two higher up, or lower down."

"But we've been four hours getting here, and have come but four miles, you think; and have four more to go, you say!"

"Well, no man need expect to see the falls of the Blackwater without some sharp walking. A mile or a mile and a half an hour, in a straight line—which would make two or three, twisting about as we have to go—is about as much as we can make out here. I could have brought you a straighter course—down through the big laurel, you know, Conaway—but if ever you once got into that, we know you would be glad enough to be out again!—and so we have been trying to head the laurel as much as possible."

"Right, men—you are right," said the Signor.

"I am not so entirely certain," responded Adolphus, "but we must abide our fate now."

"Right—all right."

"I withdraw what I said, men," observed Peter, it just occurring to him that if the guides should take it into their heads to leave us, we would be in rather a bad way. "I was very much heated just now, and a good deal blown—that's the truth; and the mind, you know, Powell, will take the hue and tone of the feelings. This little rest has put it all right, though."

"Handsomely done, and philosophically accounted for."

"Move on, Powell—it's all right!"

The Signor waved his frying-pan encouragingly, and the Master blew away upon his hand-bugle. With restored spirit, the expedition once more dashed along through the forest. Up started three or four deer from the bushes, and, showing the underside white of their tails as they threw them over their backs, with a leap and a bound they were lost in the forest. Murad ran after them a little way out of the line, and pitching down presently over some rough ground, his lame leg up in the air, he laughed out his "Ugh–uh!" and gave up the chase, saying, as he fell into line again —

"They are monstrous swift. How the fury they get over the rough ground so fast, I can't see!"

"They were born so," replied old Conway.

"It's a gift to them," said Powell. "Every animal has his gift. It's their protection. The bear climbs, and the deer runs."

The hunters discoursing their lore of the forest, we came down to the edge of some swampy ground, and found ourselves in front of a wide stretch of laurel, tangled and thick everywhere around. To cross it—as it was clear it could not be avoided in any way—the hunters looked about for the best place to go in. At length, finding a spot that bid the fairest, they made their way into the brake, and desperately after them we all followed, as best we could. Such pulling and tugging—such twisting, plunging, breaking, crashing, and tearing—

"I never remember ever to have heard" —

or seen. Here was one held fast by his wallet, and twisting about like an eel to get himself loose; there another who had got upon a huge fallen tree—thus avoiding the laurel by walking along its surface as far as it reached through the swamp; but it was so decomposed, that presently he sank into it up to his arms—and he was stuck. Here another who had reached a stream, walking in it as far as in its windings it kept a course that corresponded with our direction. There one grown entirely desperate, and endeavoring to break his way through by main strength. The hunters took it more knowingly, and would search about for the thinnest places—sometimes going back upon their tracks when they would get into a very thick part of the brake, and trying it another way.

To tell how at last we all did get out, overtaxes any powers of description that I possess. Peter succeeded eventually, and threw himself down on the ground entirely exhausted, murmuring something about *the other side of Jordan*, and the laurel being *a hard road to travel.*

The Prior came ashore with his big knife open in his hand, having at length,—like Wit in Moore's song—"*cut* his bright way through." How Triptolemus got through has never yet been fairly ascertained; but it is believed by the whole expedition that he fell through the most of the way—for whenever we had any glimpse of him, his head was down and his feet up. Somehow or other the passage was successfully accomplished; and, after resting sufficiently, we took up the line of march, with a unanimous request of the guides that they would avoid all the laurel that it was possible, by any skill of their woodcraft, to get round.

"And this is the beautiful rhododendron, Adolphus, that you and I have been trying so hard to grow," said the Master.

"I'll pull it all up as soon as I get home," replied Galen spitefully—"if, indeed, I shall ever see that blessed spot again."

"No—I'll now have a thicket of it at the Priory, if it is only that I may be able to demonstrate, when I grow old, the miracles I shall recount of this expedition."

"A good idea," said the artist. "I'll make a grand national painting of it, and call it 'The Passage of the Laurel.'"

"And hang it up by Leutze's 'Passage of the Delaware.'"

"Couldn't you put Fairfax's stone somewhere in the picture?" inquired Trip.

"Oh, certainly," returned the Signor, "and draw you, Trip, pitching into it!"

"Have Butcut stuck up to his shoulders in a decomposed hemlock, and a bear after him!"

"A rattlesnake, too!"

"A panther or so!"

"And some owls about!"

"I'll try and do the subject justice, gentlemen," replied the Signor. "No historical feature shall be left out."

Thus commenting on the passage of the laurel, we moved on; and after a while, descending a long hillside, we came to the head of a glade, through which a stream of some size ran—its waters of a light-chocolate hue. We were very much jaded by this time; and so we threw ourselves down upon the soft, beautiful grass, knee-high everywhere around, and for half an hour enjoyed such grateful rest as seldom comes to the sons and daughters of men who stay in civilized regions; it recompensed even the laurel, so exquisite was the rest, and so gorgeous the bower where we took it!

> "And then he said, 'How sweet it were
> A fisher or a hunter here,
>   A gardener in the shade,
> Still wand'ring with an easy mind
> To build a household fire, and find
>   A home in every glade!
>
> " 'What days and what sweet years!—Ah me!
> Our life were life indeed, with thee
>   So passed in quiet bliss,
> And all the while,' said he, 'to know
> That we were in a world of wo,
>   On such an earth as this!'

"And then he sometimes interwove
  Fond thoughts about a father's love:
   ' For there,' said he, 'are spun
  Around the heart such tender ties,
  That our own children to our eyes
   Are dearer than the sun.

" ' Sweet Ruth! And could you go with me,
  My helpmate in the woods to be,
   Our camp at night to rear —
  Or run, my own adopted bride,
  A sylvan huntress at my side,
   And drive the flying deer!'

" ' Beloved Ruth!' " —

Such thoughts filled the teeming brain of the Prior, as he lay sleeping in the beautiful glade.—But we can not follow him in his dreams of wild bliss; for we must go into another chapter, and bivouac for the night.

CHAPTER IX.

THE LODGE IN THE WILDERNESS.

⊷ ⚌◆⚌ ⊶

W<small>HILE</small> yet the sun in his westward journey had but about an hour to go, before he left the Canaan to darkness and the expedition—not to mention the bears and owls, &c., about—a snake stole into our bower, and disturbed the heavenly repose of the glade. A very harmless, inoffensive little grass-snake—polished and slippery, disturbed by the rolling about of some one of the party, wound itself along swiftly over one of the extended arms of Doctor Blandy, as he lay sprawled out upon his back—gazing up into the heavens, and dreaming dreams of the balmy summer's eve. Galen sprang to his feet, and jumped some ten paces off into the meadow. Whereupon we all did the same. It was a rattlesnake at least to our startled imagination!—until we saw, to our shame, that it was not. Being on our feet, however, the word was given to take up the line of march again—and off we went: the guides being of opinion, that by crossing the ridge before us, we would come upon the Blackwater by night.

We made our way out of the glade, encountering but a small strip of laurel; and once more filed into the dense wild forest. As we advanced we grew more and more silent. We were evidently beginning to flag in spirit. It was our first day, and we were not yet inured to the toil. Every now and then some startled deer would give a little life to the party—but it would not last, and we trudged along almost noiseless over the mossy ground. Instead of the country's giving indication of our being near a stream such as the Blackwater, it was growing more hilly and broken ever since we left the glade. The shades of evening too, were fast closing in upon us. Something was wrong—we ought certainly to have reached the Blackwater before this. The hunters were evidently in doubt about their course, and they now held frequent consultations with each other. They had told us before we set off from the dale of the Potomac, that they would certainly take us to our destination by night, and they were anxious to accomplish their purpose; they feared their skill as guides would be called in question if they failed in what they had been so certain of accomplishing. It was now near sundown, and we were hemmed in, on all sides, by mountains. The impression that we were really lost was uppermost in the minds of all of us; and presently we held a general council—the result of which was, that if we did not come to some indication of the Blackwater, when we crossed the next ridge, we would encamp for the night.

Crossing over this ridge, everything looked as before. It was all the same rugged, dense, dark, deep, grand gloom of mountainous forest that we had left behind us—no appearance of laurel—the sure harbinger of water; no such sloping down of the hills anywhere, as looked like the descent into a valley, such as a stream of any size would find its way through; and above all, listen as intently as we might, no sound of a waterfall (such as we were assured would greet our ears from the river we sought) was mingled with the song of the evening wind. Therefore there was but one voice in the general assembly of the expedition—and that was to halt for the night, and take counsel of to-morrow's sun as to our direction. Finding a little trickling rill in the bed of a rugged ravine close at hand, we resolved upon taking up our abode by its waters for the night. Accordingly the most appropriate spot we could find was selected; and, throwing down our burdens in a pile, we commenced the construction of a camp, with a great deal of busy bustle. As the reader unacquainted with the ways of a wilderness life, may take some interest in knowing how this was done, we will enter, for his benefit, into the particulars.

In the first place, then, the hunters set to work and gathered together a number of dried logs and limbs of trees, that they found scattered about the forest, making a pile some ten or twelve feet long, and three or four feet high. They then picked out the driest bark and branches of pine they could find, and laid them about through the pile. Next they raised some fire by striking sparks from the flints of their rifles into tow, and carefully applying this to the pine bark and other combustible wood they had gathered; it was not long before we had our wood-pile in a blaze—which was soon increased into a spreading and swelling flame, by the young hemlocks and fir trees that we were busily engaged for some time in cutting down and throwing upon the pile.

While a part of the force were engaged in this work, others were busy in arranging the camp. The ground was cleared away in front of the fire, and this place was covered over with the softest branches of hemlock that we could gather—two of the party being out cutting for the purpose. A large log was brought and laid along the back of the camp, and this was covered over to the height of two or three feet with hemlock and fir branches, serving as a sort of wall to protect us from any intrusion from that side, of beasts, or what not, that might be disposed to invade us during the night. The camp was so arranged, that when we slept, our heads would be against this barrier, and our feet to the fire. The sides also were filled up between the trees with branches. When it was all completed, we had a tenement—a lodge in the wilderness—the ground floor of which was hemlock branches a foot deep, three sides, also, hemlock and fir, and the fourth side a wood-pile, twelve feet long, four feet high, and all afire. And the roof above us:—

" ' Tis the blue vault of heaven, with its crescent so pale,
And all its bright spangles—quoth Allen-a-Dale!"

and where will you find a grander in a king's palace.

Our rifles, bags of provisions, coffee-pot, tin-cups, and frying-pan—all we had, were safely deposited in one corner of the lodge. The wallets were unrolled, and the blankets, great coats, &c., &c.—including the knives and pistols, were thrown out for use. Having cut down as many small trees as would serve to keep the fire going for the night, we now assembled in the camp, and commenced preparations for supper, for which we were by this time about as ravenous as the beasts of a menagerie about feeding time. The bread, biscuits, and cold ham, were brought forth. The sugar was untied. Conway sat about preparing the coffee: Powell started the frying-pan on the hot embers, and soon had it hissing and crackling with the slices of fat middling of bacon with which he filled it; until at length the more delicate aroma of the hemlock was lost to our noses, in the ascendency of the bacon-side.

Those of us who were not engaged in these enticing preparations, were lying about on the hemlock, enjoying ourselves in the abandonment of forest undress—that is, in our stocking feet, with ungirded vest, unsuspendered; and spread out around, in all the various attitudes that it was possible for a set of tired men to stretch themselves in. At length the supper was announced as ready—and then it was devoured.

To say that it was merely eaten up, would be a pre-
posterous defamation of any ideas of eating, such
as the word generally conveys in civilized life. In an
exceeding short space of time, of all the liberal preparation, there were, at all events, no visible evidences
remaining—except the table-service—the tin and the
iron. It was as if a set of jugglers had suddenly juggled
it out of sight—caused it all to *evanish*. It convinced
my mind more thoroughly than anything I have wit-
nessed in my somewhat varied life—that man is, by
nature, a wild beast. Reduce him into his original
elements—take off all this varnish, this overlarding
of civilization—put him out in the Canaan here for
about a month, and what beast is there of the wild
that will out-raven him! Poetry, philosophy, arts, and
science—these have humanized him; and made him,
even when he is most starved, wave his hand to this
friend, and with a smile upon his countenance, say,
Take the first grab, as did the famished Signor to the
rapacious Butcut—which made the yet unsatisfied
Blandy hand over the last slice of the middling to
lame Triptolemus, and belie himself, when he said,
Take that, Trip, I'm not a-hungry. The reader will perceive, from this, that the wilderness had not yet made
us altogether savage; also he will perceive though,
that its tendency is toward the dehumanization of
man—the resolving him into his original simple element of wild beast.

I would take advantage of this occasion—all the
great historians do so—to philosophize a little upon

the absolute necessity there is for good government over mankind—that there should be good laws, and firmly maintained—how stability and order, and the social decorums, that make nations refined and great, and keep them so, are thereby only upheld: how otherwise, man will soon convert the garden-spots of the world into a bear-walk. These high corollaries I would deduce from our experience of the wilderness, and go to the trouble of showing them convincingly, with reasons manifold, were it not, that just at this time there is a practical teaching of them everywhere over the land, that is making the lesson manifest to the dullest mind—and which practical teaching, if not arrested, will soon convert the garden of our American civilization into such a bear-walk as the world has not yet seen.

Be these things, however, as they may—let the republic tremble to its foundations, if it must—let political and social anarchy take it, if it has to be so—there are those about who will right it, and rear its firm head higher, and higher yet, to the skies. In the meantime, when the hurly-burly comes, we of this expedition have made up our minds to seize upon the Canaan; and with the knowledge we have acquired of its fastnesses—such as the laurel:—its gorges, narrow defiles, rocky precipices, and torrent passes—all its military availabilities—it will go hard with us if we don't hold it against all the other freebooters of the United States—let their name be legion!

However, upon this point we must keep our counsel, or we might be frustrated in our enterprise by the rapine of the times. *A wise man is his own lantern.*

In the meantime, the supper was gone—juggled, or jugged away; and the animals to all appearances appeased. We now gathered into the inner penetralia of our hold; and stowed ourselves away in every violation of the rules of ceremony known to any of the nations of Christendom, or of the heathen—smoking cigars or pipes—telling stories, and singing songs, of love, war, romance, the chase, intermixed with our national anthems, and local ballads, pathetic or humorous, now in the harmony of Germany or of Italy, of France or old romantic Spain, and now to the strains of some low, dulcet, African refrain. Thus were passed the first watches of the night, until, at length, tired nature yielded to the omnipotence of sleep; and, hushed by the night winds murmuring among the immemorial trees, while the blazing pile at our feet illumined the forest around and above us with its silver and golden flame, imparting a magic sheen to the leaves and branches of the woods, until it all seemed the lighted tracery of some vast Gothic minster of the wild; and with nothing above us but the vault of heaven, studded with its glittering stars (which we couldn't see)—and nothing beneath us but the spicy smelling hemlock—and nothing over us but a blanket—we fell asleep, as sweetly and confidingly here in the wild, as children beneath the roof-tree of some guardian home.

And so, tired reader, good night! May your sleep be ever as safe in the city, and your dreams never worse than those that haunted the hemlock of our lost expedition.

CHAPTER X.

THE BLACKWATER FOUND—A GREAT NUMBER OF TROUT TAKEN—MR. BUTCUT FRIES SOME FISH.

ABOUT daybreak, when our sleep was at the highest, and the atmosphere the most chilly—the twilight just emerging from the night—Doctor Adolphus Blandy awoke from his dreams. Sleeping next to Mr. Butcut—and that gentleman, taking good care of himself even in his sleep, having contrived to appropriate to himself, during the night, the blanket that warmed the shoulders of Adolphus—the doctor woke up at this hour yawning and chilled. Contemplating for a while, the comfortable party around him, and particularly contemplating the exceedingly comfortable Butcut, just at this time emitting the longest drawn and most swelling notes of his horn; and also reflecting, and, somewhat bitterly may be, that all this was doubly enjoyed by But, at the expense of his own shivering discomfort—himself sacrificed to this too complete bodily satisfaction of the partner of his sleep—and accustomed, no doubt, himself to his own proper share of nocturnal indulgence: thus contemplating the repose around him, the devil of that dog-in-the-manger quality of our nature, that will sometimes get uppermost in the breasts of the best of men, arose and took possession of his soul.

"Aha, Mr. But!" said Galen to himself, "you look mighty comfortable, indeed, with every bit of my blanket wrapped about you—tucked in, too! No wonder I couldn't pull it over me. I'll fix you, Mr. Snug, for this, I think. If I'm shivering here, you sha'n't sleep so comfortably there, and in my blanket, too—confound you!"

So he deliberately arose, and set fire to the hemlock upon which we were sleeping, starting the flame at a point nearest to the object of his particular malice. Having got his blaze under way, he next picked up a hatchet, and finding a young fir-tree so placed that when cut down it would fall with all its branches directly upon the sleepers, he went to work to fell it, a great deal of especial delight beaming all the while from his eyes.

The hemlock being of the Pinus species, fire takes hold of it rapidly, and soon the camp was in a blaze. The flames spreading in close proximity around Peter, crackling upon his ear, and flaring in his eye, he awoke in great terror, and aroused the camp with his outcries. Just at this critical moment, down came the doctor's young fir-tree, that he had been all the while industriously hacking at, down right over the camp, with all its sweeping branches, trapping the party. Of course, there was no little commotion among us. The fire was instantly put out, however, by a sort of instinct of preservation common to mankind; and not yet fairly awake, and a general impression prevailing in the confusion that we were attacked by the wild animals, we seized upon the rifles, hatchets, knives, frying-pan, and but-ends of the burned wood-pile, to sell our lives as dearly as possible. Missing Blandy, however, who had concealed himself behind a tree, the reality of the case began to break upon us; and fairly now awake, we commented variously upon the caricature alacrity that had been exhibited by the expedition in defending itself from the supposed assault of the beasts of the wilderness—and took advantage of the occasion to get breakfast, and make an early start for the day.

The breakfast was a repetition of the last night's supper, which being said—it is enough. Presently the sun reddened the eastern sky, and the hunters getting the direction they proposed to try their fortune in, we set off through the yet dank and dewy forest. Our way was broken and rugged, up and down, through ravines that were deep chasms, and over great fallen trees covered with moss and wet as a sponge. Deer we saw frequently browsing about, and out here where perhaps they had never seen a human being before, they would lift up their heads and for a while gaze at us as if in wonder at what it all meant. Once or twice it was proposed to shoot one of them, but this was cried down as an act of wantonness, since we were already burdened with as much as we could carry; and, uncertain as to our being at all in the right direction, we were somewhat anxious and desirous to hasten on our way, while yet fresh from the night's rest.

There was one part of the wilderness which we traversed this morning, where we came frequently upon the traces of bear. Sometimes we would come upon the trunk of a dead tree, some hundred feet long, and five or six feet in diameter, scattered and raked about in all directions by the bears to get at the worms to eat. Sometimes we would find a cluster of trees, with the bark worn smooth, which the hunters told us was a certain indication that a family of these animals had been here raised, and were no doubt now in some hollow tree or fastness not far off.

Thus we walked along for several hours, probably at no greater rate than a mile an hour, and in some evident disheartenment—for we were not at all so light of spirit as we might have been, and would, had we felt more certain of our course. Every now and then when we stopped to rest, the conversation would take a debating turn, the subject discussed being generally the points of the compass; one asserting that here was the north, and another that it was in the very opposite direction. Peter's mind was always opposed to the hunters'; if they pointed this way for north, he was sure to point in the opposite, and maintain his point of the compass with much vehement speech; for he was by this time fully assured that the hunters had no knowledge of the country—in fact knew nothing of wood-craft at all. These debates were generally wound up by some very direct remark of Triptolemus's, proclaiming it as his opinion, that the hunters didn't know any more than he did, where we were—when some one of the more discreet members of the party would have to intimate to Powell and Conway, that Trip didn't mean as much as he said, for fear they might possibly lose their good temper, and leave the whole expedition in the lurch, by deserting us upon the first favorable opportunity: in which event it is altogether likely we would have remained out in the Canaan long enough to have resolved ourselves into our original wild elements, or to have become a pile of bones. But Powell and Conway were good-tempered men, and set down to the proper account all our insinuations against their knowledge; and generally retired to a little distance, and held some rational parley with each other upon the matter in doubt.

At length we scrambled up a desperate hill, and seating ourselves down to rest on its brow, we heard Peter's voice back in the bushes, crying out that he couldn't stand it any longer. Presently he came in, out of breath, dragging himself along; and sitting down on a log with an air of dogged resolution, great misery in his countenance, he swore he would go no further.

"Gentlemen, there must be an end put to this. I can't stand it. It's all intolerable—terrific!"

"Let him stay here, then," said the Signor. "We'll go on, and find the falls. We can then send one of the men back for him."

The enterprise was growing desperate, so we moved along, determined to find water at all hazards, if we fell in our tracks. As we took up the march again, each man gave Peter a parting volley.

"You had better struggle on, But, as long as you can. If you should be left here, you will never find the way in yourself."

"And bear it in mind, an expedition fitted out for your recovery might not be more fortunate than those to the North Pole."

"And, But, there is a possibility that government mightn't think you worth discovering."

"Mr. Grinnell couldn't be calculated on for you, Peter."

"And if ever you are found, you might be a pile of bones—remember the lost man!" said Trip.

"Farewell, Peter! I'm sorry to leave you, old fellow."

"Go to—," said Peter, "with your blasted nonsense. Since you won't stop and encamp, I'll show you I can walk with any of you."

And Peter got up and followed after, not liking the idea of remaining by himself in the forest; and thinking rightly it would be rather hazardous to be left behind by the party.

About an hour after this we were walking along the broad top of a ridge, when one of the hunters stopped, and thought he heard something like the distant sound of water. Reanimated by the thought we pricked up our ears, and went on in better heart. But Botecote, who was really suffering a good deal, now came to a dead halt, and refused to move. No persuasion this time, nor any banter—no argument addressed to his hopes, nor any intimidation of any sort, that the inventive genius of the expedition could suggest—was of the least avail. The case this time was desperate; and we held a council of war over him, the chief question being what was to be done with his body. He was too big to carry—which was the suggestion of Triptolemus—so, of course, that thought was dismissed; and, besides, we had no idea of doing it: for we had still a lurking belief that he was playing 'possum a little, in order that he might accomplish an encampment. Fortunately, however, and saving us from the desperate measure of leaving him here in the forest, with a chance that we should not be able to find him again, old Conway had explored the side of the mountain, and just now returned, saying that he had come to a wide belt of laurel, and that it was his opinion the Blackwater ran through it.

"I knew it," said Peter. "It's just as I said, gentlemen. We've been enduring all this horrible walking all the morning, when, by going more to the left, we might have been in the Blackwater long ago. Walked to death for nothing!"

And now it was suggested that the laurel should be explored, the fact of the water ascertained, and Peter put into it, to make his way to the falls down the middle of the stream. This proposition was assented to, as the best the case admitted of. Accordingly, going down to the edge of the laurel, and seeing Peter safely deposited in the brake—with some appropriate encouragement of him as he fought his way through—and hearing presently his somewhat cheerful shout, announcing his safe arrival in the stream—we made our way back again to the top of the mountain—Powell being certain now that we were on the Blackwater, and that in the course of a mile or so we would come upon some of its falls. Indeed, we were now convinced that we heard the sound of them in the distance.

We pursued our march along the cone of the ridge we were on for something better than a mile, when, coming to a halt, we distinctly heard a waterfall below us. There was no doubt about it now: and we descended the mountain-side with a shout. We met the laurel about half-way down the mountain—and breaking into it, after the necessary fighting, we filed down, one by one, along a great fir-tree that had, happily for us, fallen there some ten or twenty years before, and stepped out into the Blackwater, on a broad surface of rock—the very top itself of the falls we were seeking. In a few minutes we fixed up our fishing-lines, and, dotted along the edge of the fall which was about ten feet high, middle of the day as it was when the fish generally cease to bite, we took from the pool below some sixty trout, as fast as we could bait our hooks for them. Satisfied with this taste of the stream, and assured of our hopes of trout innumerable, we descended the falls, and looked about for a suitable spot to construct a camp, and prepare our dinner—for which, by this time, we were in no little need, having eaten nothing since the early twilight.

In the meantime, Mr. Butcut and Conway—fishing down the middle of the stream, and having caught some thirty or forty more trout as they came along—arrived at the falls, and thus the party were once more together—boastful over all our toil and suffering, and in high and happy spirits at the successful achievement of the enterprise out.

In the course of an hour a camp was constructed by the banks of the stream, about a hundred yards below the falls. A great blazing fire, such as we had the night before, was soon under way; and lazily stretched about on the hemlock, or out upon the large, moss-covered rocks that bordered the stream—now frying and eating a pan of trout at returning intervals, as a not quite sated appetite prompted, or taking a little sleep, as nature inclined—we passed the hours until about four o'clock, when it was deemed advisable to sally forth for the purpose of laying in provision for our supper and the next morning's breakfast.

Leaving some of the party to perfect the works at the camp, and make everything as comfortable as possible for the night, we divided the rest into two bands, and set out—one up the stream, the other down—to make a somewhat extensive foray upon the trout.

We will not give a minute account of the evening's fishing. We will state generally that the inroad was very successful; that we took the trout as fast as we could bait for them; that in a walk of about a mile up the stream, and two miles down, and back, we at length arrived in camp with about as many fish as we could well carry—and were back all of us about an hour before dark, and all rather indifferent about taking any more trout that evening.

Immediately in front of the camp, and about a step out in the stream, is a large rock, in shape a parallelogram, of some five feet by ten, rising above the water about three feet, and of almost an entirely flat surface, except where at one end it is scooped into a slight hollow, that will hold some two or three buckets of water. This rock we have appropriated as our kitchen; and upon it we have counted out some five hundred trout, varying in size from six to ten inches—some of them, the black trout, with deep red spots—and some salmon-colored, with lighter red spots—all of them very beautiful, though not, of course, of the largest size of the fish; for we have yet to go down below the great falls of the Blackwater to get at them.

All hands are now called into requisition to clean all these fish; and it is not long before the whole five hundred are prepared for the pan, and safely put away in the hollow basin at the other end of the kitchen, with a plenty of good fresh water around them.

By the side of this rock, called the kitchen, a little farther out in the stream—an easy step taking you from the top of the kitchen-rock to it—is another large sandstone rock, which is our parlor. This last is about ten feet by twelve, and about three feet also above the water, and perfectly flat and smooth on its surface. Describing thus our different apartments—all, like the statues of the heathen goddesses in the "Groves of Blarney," standing out "naked in the open air"—perhaps it would afford the reader some satisfaction to know our manner of using them. It is very simple; as thus:—

You will have the goodness to observe the movements of Mr. Butcut at this moment. This gentleman has a turn for good living, and consequently he is something of an amateur cook. Indeed, it is his pleasure so to indulge his genius this way, that after he has himself eaten as much as he wants for the time being, he takes great delight in exercising his talents for the gratification of others. He is now about to cook a mess for the Prior, who, coming in the last from fishing, has now made himself ready to enjoy his supper, having a very fine rage upon him at present, and a particularly good capacity at all times to go upon. Butcut takes up the frying-pan, and repairs with it to the kitchen. Placing it down by the fish, he selects from the clean and beautiful hundreds in the basin about eight fine fish—half of them black, half of them salmon-colored, all of them of the largest and fattest—these being just as many as the bottom of the frying-pan will properly hold. He takes them carefully, even daintily, by the tail, between his fore-finger and thumb, and places them accurately in the pan in alternate heads and tails. A little salt and a little black pepper are carefully sprinkled over them. He next cuts a few thin slices of middling of bacon and places them about in the pan. He is now ready for the fire. So he goes to the great blazing pile, and raking out from underneath it, away from any smoke, a quantity of the livest embers, he sets the frying-pan evenly on these, and soon has the whole delicate mess frying away in the most delightful manner—the fat of the middling crackling and hissing a most delicious music to his ear—also to the ear of the expectant Master. The accomplished Peter takes great care that the fish shall not burn in the least, so he removes the pan from the hot embers every once in a while. Cooked sufficiently now, as he supposes, on the one side, he proceeds to the operation of turning them. This he does after the manner of tossing a pancake. He spreads a white napkin upon the rock hard by, and giving the frying-pan a toss of a very artful character, up go the trout in the air, turning over and coming down into the pan again precisely as the arch-cook desires it: and all this is done without spilling even so much as a drop of grease on the napkin. He now goes to the fire again, and performs some more hocus-pocus, that is all Hebrew-Greek to the ignorant, until the mess is of a delicate brown hue—when he deems the operation complete, and hands the frying-pan to the Master with an air which seems to say, "A dish fit to set before a king!"

The sharp-set Prior, in the meantime, has prepared himself with a plate—of the real stone-ware—that is, a flat, thin stone, of some twelve inches' diameter, which he has selected from the bed of the stream for his purpose; and emptying the trout upon his plate, with a chunk of bread on one end of it and his big knife on the other, he hands the frying-pan to the next gentleman eagerly waiting for it, and proceeds from the fireplace to the kitchen, and from the kitchen to the parlor, where he sets himself down, with his legs crossed under him after the fashion of the Grand Mufti, and, with his plate before him, dips in, and makes away with the spoils of the Blackwater, in what in elegant life would be considered a very short space of time, but which excites no comment at all out here—it being common to all the men we have seen feed in the country.

The trout is such light food, that eight of them, some ten inches long, will not make a supper for a hearty man, leading this wilderness life; and accordingly the Master asks for another plateful. But Mr. Butcut is by this time cooking another little mess for himself, his appetite getting up again on him: so the former gentleman has to wait for his turn at the frying-pan, and try his hand for himself.

But enough. This will suffice to show the habits of our indoor life out here on the Blackwater—and give also some very just idea of the different apartments of our dwelling, and of our felicitous manner of using them.

CHAPTER XI.

THE BLACKWATER VILLA.

O<small>UR</small> Blackwater villa is placed in the most picturesque position imaginable—almost immediately upon the banks of the most lovely of all amber streams. It is protected on one side by masses of gray sandstone rock, dashed with spots of a darker and lighter hue of gray, and occasionally a tinge of red—these rocks coated over in places with moss of various mingled colors—gray, blue, green, yellow, and purple, and soft and glossy as the richest velvet. A noble overshadowing fir-tree rises up from one corner of the villa, some hundred and fifty feet, to the skies. The laurel grows thick and matted back of it, in impenetrable masses; and the glory of its flower, now just swelling into bloom, gives an air of elegance—even of splendor, to the embowered dwelling. In front, the pure cool stream leaps over the falls like a river of calf's-foot jelly with a spray of whipped syllabub on top of it, and tumbles wildly down through its rocky and obstructed bed, filling your imagination with the poetry of unpolluted mountain waters—running pure to your ideal, as the kingdom of heaven.

The valley of the Blackwater is not more than a hundred yards wide, here where we have made our home; and embowered on all sides, by mountains of noble forms and various, it wears an air of entire seclusion from the world we have deserted. No intruding footsteps of man, we instinctively feel, will here disturb our chosen, perfect solitude. All customs, manners, modes of life, that we have heretofore known, are felt to be the remembrance of an almost forgotten dream. The earth is entirely new to our senses; and it is all our own—an entire and absolutely perfect fee-simple estate of inheritance in land and water, the deed recorded in the most secret recesses of our own breasts. Therefore we feel an unbounded liberty of thought, speech, and action, and this is manifest in all we say and do; and hence the reader will easily understand how it is, that there is such entire freedom of remark among us, one to another; how it is that we lay about on the hemlock, now that night has set in upon us, in such careless luxuriance of attitude; how that the Prior is now stretched out with his feet to the fire, and one of the hunters squatted down confidingly between them; how the Signor goes on all fours over our bodies, in getting to a snug place in a corner of the camp, whither his fancy now urges him; how that Mr. Butcut is flat upon his back in the middle of the softest hemlock, his face direct to the heavens, and his body spread out as usual in his favorite position of a supple-jack distorted to the utmost; how Triptolemus's lame leg is thrown over one of old Conway's shoulders, with a view to the convenient drying of a wet stocking before the fire; how it is that Adolphus, with a blanket sweeping his shoulders, half sits, half reclines in among the roots of the great fir-tree, wishing he could smoke a mild Havana like the rest of us—but compensating his soul for his inability, by indulging in visions of trout swimming about in all beautiful imaginary waters—the day-dream haunting the lights and shadows of his face like an angel of Paradise.

Lying about thus in all unrestrained felicity, we told stories, and discoursed much learning of the fisherman and the hunter, ancient and modern; every now and then interweaving some very entertaining and free—sometimes very slashing comment upon one another; all of which we regret it is out of the question for us to impart to the reader, because of its too great freedom, even for this outspoken age. Herein, therefore, that we may not fall below the dignity of history—having pitched our chronicle up to the very highest standard—we must exercise a becoming self-denial, hard as it is to refrain.

The moon has now risen, and although a few light fleecy clouds are gathering about here and there above us, yet the goddess of the night shines down as silvery soft upon the Canaan, as she did of old upon the garden of Verona, where Lorenzo and Jessica vied with each other in chanting her worship in such beautiful strains. And, oh! most beautiful reader—now absorbing this inspired chapter, like Geraldine, when in her night-robes loose, she lay reclined on couch of Ind, and poured over Surrey's raptured line—how soothingly soft its influence upon us here in the wild, you—you can never altogether know—not even from this rapt page!—how all at once, as if at another Prospero's wand, our mood was changed from that of wanton, reckless mirth, and a gentle dreamy inspiration, all poetry and romance (all the finer for our satisfaction in the regard of the trout—heavenly fish!)—came with the balmy south wind, and took possession of our souls! You—even you, blissful girl, upon whom the favoring gods have bestowed the gift of genius, as well as of beauty—you, with your "finely-fibred frame," like Georgiana's, duchess of Devonshire, whom Coleridge has so finely commemorated in his beautiful lines addressed to that lady—even you can not ever know this, unless, perchance, you would go with me, and live a sylvan huntress by my side in the Canaan, as did Ruth with her roving lover in the wilds of Georgia! But God temper the wind to you, shorn lamb, if you should ever trust yourself to my freebooter's faith!—unless, indeed, a latent Helen MacGreggor might be contained in your inches!

The moon and the soft south wind held us now completely enthralled in their divine ravishment;

and in this mood we grew musical—the Signor Andante at length tuning his voice to the beautiful serenade of Henry Neele: perhaps the most exquisite
song that has yet been composed by any of our coun-
trymen. It was thus Andante's voice, murmured a
music sweeter than the Blackwater in our ears:—

THE SERENADE.

"Wake, lady, wake—the midnight moon
  Sails through the cloudless skies of June:
  The stars gaze sweetly on the stream
  Which, in the brightness of their beam,
    One sheet of glory lies.
  The glow-worm lends its little light,
  And all that's beautiful and bright
  Is shining on our world to-night,
    Save thy bright eyes!

"Wake, lady, wake—the nightingale
  Tells to the moon her love-lorn tale!
  Now doth the brook that's hushed by day,
  As through the vale she winds her way
    In murmurs sweet rejoice;
  The leaves by the soft night-wind stirred,
  Are whispering many a gentle word,
  And all earth's sweetest sounds are heard
    Save thy sweet voice!

"Wake, lady, wake—thy lover waits,
  Thy steed stands saddled at the gates!
  Here is a garment rich and rare,
  To wrap thee from the cold night air;
    The appointed hour is flown—
  Danger and doubt have vanished quite
  Our way before is clear and bright—

And all is ready for the flight—
   Save thou alone!

"Wake, lady, wake—I have a wreath,
   Thy broad, fair brow shall rise beneath:
   I have a ring that must not shine
   On any finger, love, but *thine!*
      I've kept my plighted vow.
   Beneath thy casement here I stand,
   To lead thee by thy own white hand,
   Far from this dull and captive strand—
      But *where art thou?*"

The last notes of the serenade died away upon the air; and not a sound disturbed the repose of the wilderness, save the murmur of the waters, and the whisperings of the trees. Each one of us, according to his gifts, was enjoying a little world of romance of his own—his soul lapped up in the creations of his gently-inspired brain—thinking not at all of the external world, but only of the ideal, conjured up by his teeming, beguiling fancy; when all at once a sudden blow sprung up fitfully out of the stillness of the air, and threw the whole forest in commotion. The fire at our feet shot up a startling blaze, in among the branches of the piled-up fir and hemlock hitherto untouched, and the crackling flames, with their myriad spangles, rose high aloft in spiral curls, almost up to the overhanging branches of the forest. Startled out of all the glory of our visioned romance, we arose and looked out upon the night. Clouds were gathering like mustering bands everywhere in the heavens, and fast concentrating their forces.

The stars disappeared by squadrons from the just now blue and shining vault of heaven; and the fair goddess of the night, queen of the glittering realm—pale Dian, veiled her mild glories altogether from our eyes. The southwest—harbinger of summer storms, is a swift and impetuous power in the air, and wonderfully does he bestir himself sometimes. So it was with him to-night; for he sprang up suddenly upon us, without any warning, and vented himself, for some cause or other to us unknown, in outbursts of gusty bluster and passion, that made us think of a whole deluge of waters descending upon our devoted camp, drowning out our fires and drenching our very beds. But for the present there was more of bravado than performance in his high mightiness; and the storm blast blew by. Still darkness was everywhere over the face of the earth, and the forest sent forth a low wail, and the waters murmured a sullen and monotonous song—falling upon the ear more like a heavy sea breaking lazily upon a flat shore, than the light, airy, wild, sportive, notes of the playful, impetuous, young streams of the mountains.

Each man now wrapped himself around more closely in his blanket. No word was spoken, but filled with the gloom of the night, we thought wistfully of our pleasant homes—dry and snug, and of household security and comfort—books, lights, music, fruits, flowers, jocund children—that is those who had them—the sly flirtation by the light of the chandelier—

"And mama, too, blind to discover
The small white hand in mine"—

—all that makes civilization tolerable; and we out here, in the wilds of the Canaan, far away from the knowledge of men—to say nothing of women—perhaps lost—and to all reasonable certainty a night of wind and rain before us—bears, panthers, wolves, owls, around us, and may be not so far off as we might desire! The melancholy soughing of the pines, too, above all the voices of the Canaan, had entered into our hearts, and awakened our superstition, and no diversion of thought could dispossess our souls of its influence. The Master, indeed, seemed rather to encourage it; for presently from out a dark corner, where half in the glimmer of the fire and half in the gloom of the hemlock he lay propped away in a very Ossianly state of mind, in a low, wild voice, all in harmony with the soughing sound of the firs and the sullen murmur of the waters, he broke in upon the gloom of the camp, crooning the beautiful ballad of Rossmore. It was thus the mournful descant fell upon our ears—now low as the lowest moan of the pines—now rising, now swelling, as the winds blew a louder wail:—

ROSSMORE.

"The day was declining,
    The dark night drew near;
The old lord grew sadder,
    And paler with fear.
'Come hither, my daughter,
    Come nearer—oh, near!—
It's the wind or the water
    That sighs in my ear!'

"Not the wind nor the water
    Now stirred the night air,
But a warning far sadder—
    The banshee was there!
Now rising, now swelling,
    On the night wind it bore
One cadence—still telling,
    'I want thee, Rossmore!'

"And then fast came his breath,
    And more fixed grew his eye:
And the shadow of death
    Told his hour was nigh!
Ere the dawn of that morning
    The struggle was o'er,
For when thrice came the warning—
    A corpse was Rossmore!"

"Hush your horrible croaking!" said Adolphus, when the Master's voice had come to a stand-still. "Shut up, or I'll leave the room! Isn't it all miserable enough already, but you must be keeping us from going to sleep with ballads about dying men, and such unearthly things?"

"Let's put him out!" exclaimed Peter.

"Turn him out into the wilderness, and let him run with Ishmael and the other beasts!"

"Pitch him into the Blackwater!"

"And if there are any big falls below, let him go down them!"

"Kill him!—curse him—kill him!"

"I have heard about such things, Mr. Philips," said Powell—"like that about Rossmore. Do you believe in them?"

"Oh, certainly, Powell."

"I once saw a spirit," said old Conway.

"With a long tail on him?" asked Peter.

"Well, I can't say but it had," continued the old man with eagerness. "Once—it was on a dark, black—the blackest sort of a night—about the end of one November—I was a-walking alone in the woods—and I came close upon a—"

"Don't tell it—it was nothing but a bear or a wolf!" exclaimed Butcut. "I wish I was at home. What a fool I was for coming here!"—and Peter tried again to sleep.

The sobbing and sighing wind still kept up its sad lament throughout the vale; and Andante to its accompaniment again tuned his voice, and half-spoke, half-sung the following strange old Scotch ballad:—

THE TWA CORBIES.

"There were twa corbies sat on a tree,
 Large and black as black might be;
 And one the other 'gan say,
 'Where shall we go and dine to-day?
 Shall we dine by the wild salt sea?
 Shall we go dine 'neath the greenwood-tree?'

"'As I sat on the deep sea-sand,
 I saw a fair ship nigh at land:
 I waved my wings, I bent my beak—
 The ship sank, and I heard a shriek!
 There they lie, one, two, and three—
 I shall dine by the wild salt sea.'

"'Come, I will show you a sweeter sight—
 A lonesome glen and a new-slain knight:
 His blood yet on the grass is hot,
 His sword half-drawn, his shafts unshot,
 And no one kens that he lies there,
 But his hawk, his hound, and his lady-fair!

"'His hound is to the hunting gane,
 His hawk to fetch the wild-fowl hame,
 His lady's away with another mate,
 So we shall make our dinner sweet;
 Our dinner's sure, our feasting free—
 Come and dine by the greenwood-tree.

"'Ye shall sit on his white hause-bane,
 I will pick out his bonny blue e'en;
 Ye'll take a tress of his yellow hair,
 To theak your nest when it grows bare;
 The gowden down on his young chin
 Will do to sewe my young ones in.

> "'Oh, cauld and bare will his bed be,
> When winter storms sing in the tree!
> At his head a turf, at his feet a stone—
> He will sleep, nor hear the maiden's moan:
> O'er his white bones the birds shall fly,
> The wild deer bound, and foxes cry!'"

"This thing is getting intolerable!" exclaimed Galen.

"It must be put an end to!" said But.

"Perhaps," observed Guy, "you might prefer to hear the ballad of 'Harold the Grim.' That's a ballad, now, for such a night as this! I think I could pitch it to the 'Infernal Waltz' in 'Robert the Devil.' Touch us the strain, Signor."

Here the Signor let himself loose upon the waltz, and went on into the opera in general, joined at length by Mr. Butcut and our whole orchestra—Powell and Conway smoking their pipes all the while in utter amazement at the effect produced. This led to the performance of divers other pieces from the other operas, in executing which, "Harold the Grim," and the wail of the forest, and the sad murmur of the Blackwater, were all forgotten for the time.

The spirited defiance of our condition did not last. It was but a temporary rising up; and, tired out, we laid ourselves down upon the hemlock, and again gave way to the Ossianly influences of the forest. The owls by this time began to hoot about in alternate question and answer. "Whoo-whoo-whoo-whoo are you?" said one, and another answered with a hollow, short laugh—"Whoo-oo-oo-oo!—whoo-oo-oo-oo!" Certain now that the owls were beginning to come about us—attracted, no doubt, by the cooking of the camp—we expected, the next thing, to hear of the approach of the bears and panthers in our neighborhood. The smell of the bacon and grease of our kitchen would undoubtedly bring these gentlemen around us sometime in the night; it might be, indeed, that our own meat would draw them: and in the event of its turning out a night of rain, why then our fire might be drenched out, and there would be nothing to keep the animals from coming in upon us.

In the meantime, however, these thoughts naturally arising in the mind, Triptolemus lifted up his voice, and of his own accord—in a somewhat discordant tone, in keeping with the rude character of the rhythm—chanted the ditty of

BANGUM AND THE WILD-BOAR.

"There is a wild-boar in the wood,
        Killum-coo, Con!
    There is a wild-boar in the wood,
    He'll eat your meat and drink your blood—
        Cut him down!
        Cut him down!

"Bangum vowed that he would ride,
        Killum-coo, Con!
    Bangum vowed that he would ride,
    With sword and pistol by his side,
        Cut him down!
        Cut him down!

"He tracked the wild-boar to his den,
  Killum-coo, Con!
He tracked the wild-boar to his den,
And there he saw the bones of ten thousand men,
  Cut him down!
  Cut him down!

"They fought three hours by the day,
  Killum-coo, Con!
They fought three hours by the day,
Till at last the wild-boar—he *ran away*,
  Cut him down!
  Cut him down!"

This delightful ballad of "Bangum and the Boar" Trip sang all to himself, for by this time we were about getting to sleep. Whether this version is a correct one, Heaven only knows! But we give it here as Trip sang it, and the probability therefore is that it is a good deal mixed up. Be this as it may, it is a very remarkable lyric, and worthy of being preserved in this chronicle as a specimen of our earlier and ruder song.

About this time some drops of rain fell down heavily upon the leaves of the forest—premonitory of what was in store for us; and in five minutes more, we, our camp, and everything around, were drenched. As it seemed to be a rather settled, steady pouring down of the clouds, without any wind or noise of any sort about it—and as there was no help for it, the hunters secured the fire as well as they could (covering it over partially with some pieces of hemlock-bark); when, rooting ourselves about among each other like a litter of pigs in a barnyard, we soon fell asleep, in defiance of the pitiless elements.

CHAPTER XII.

THE FALLS OF THE BLACKWATER.

Undisturbed by any of the wild beasts, we slept through the rain until broad daylight, when we crawled out of our litter, and started the nearly-extinguished fire. The rain had ceased to fall sometime in the night; but the mist covered the mountains and enveloped the river; the forest was everywhere dripping wet, and for a while it was rather cheerless as we sat drooping before the slow fire. Soon, however, the flames took hold of the wood, and, as the blaze spread, our spirits revived.

The worst possible thing for a man to do, under any circumstances, is to sit down and droop: the very best, all the philosophers agree, is to go to work. So we picked up the hatchets and axe, and soon had a wagon-load of young hemlocks and firs upon the fire, making a flame that dried the atmosphere all around our villa. In doing this, it was discovered that we were as supple of joint and limb as if we had slept in moonshine; and when Triptolemus looked for his cold (which he had brought with him into the country), and couldn't find it—and Mr. Butcut felt himself lighter and freer in body than he had done since he started—it would have puzzled any one, coming fresh among us, to believe that we had slept out all night in the open air, in a drenching rain.

After breakfast, however, going beyond the encampment, and seeing everything still wet and uncomfortable, the hearts of some of the party began to fail them—and it was proposed that we should strike our camp for home.

"What! and not explore the stream, after coming out all the way here for the purpose!—No—not so," said the artist, who wished to sketch the falls.

"Not so," repeated the Master, who wished to take some of the larger trout of the Blackwater.

"And you mean, then, to keep us out here another night in the rain!" exclaimed Peter. "I won't submit to it!"

"I should rather think we have had enough of it," said Galen—the idea of another night of rain destroying his romance a little.

"What do you say, Trip? Are you satisfied?"

"Ugh—uh!" replied Trip; but whether he meant yes or no, was only to be got at from his countenance—which was rather down.

"It will read badly in our annals, gentlemen," observed the Master, "to go back without exploring the falls. Besides, I want to get in among the large fish. We have caught nothing to call a trout yet!"

"We have seen all the falls we are going to see," said Peter.

"What's your opinion as to that, Powell?"

"There are certainly larger falls, gentlemen, somewhere down below us. These couldn't make all the roar we have heard out here—could they, Conaway?"

"That's onpossible," replied Conway.

"Gentlemen, I am really suffering very much out here—this climate don't agree with me!" said Peter, pathetically.

"You look ill, But!"

Peter smiled faintly at this. It was the first trace of anything of the kind that had illumined his countenance since day dawned.

The reader will perceive, from the above conversation—which will serve as a sample of a very considerable discussion, involving the breaking up of the expedition at this point—that some of us had enough of the wilderness. Although we were all perfectly unharmed by the exposure of the last night, yet the recollection of it affected the mind unpleasantly, and suggested visions of the comfort of Towers's hostel, which made against any very strong wish to remain out another night—such night in our Blackwater villa. But the secret of this desire to leave was attributable to the fact that the sun had not yet risen high enough to clear the hilltops, and disperse the mists and fogs of the morning, which after such a night of rain, had enveloped everywhere the beautiful world around. Let but the sun shine awhile,

and the glory of the rhododendron—the beauty of
light and shade—the splendor of the living green of
the wild—the sheen and the sparkle of the waters—
the summer-morning breeze—the song of the birds—
all the glories of the month of June in the mountains—all these must enter into the heart, and bring
gladness to despair itself. As it was, the Master and
the Signor rather had But, and Galen, and Trip, in
their power; for the two hunters, it was very evident,
were keen-set for the exploration of the falls. No one
up here knew anything about these falls, other than
the conjecture of their existence: at any rate, there
was no known man who had seen them. The pride of
discovery, therefore, operated on the hunters; and it
was apparent that all Andante and the Master had
to do, was to say the word, and they couldn't be
bribed to go back. However, the sun began to shine
out about this time, breaking through the mists of
the valley; and it was agreed that the exploring party
should go out, while the others would amuse themselves fishing or shooting in the neighborhood of the
camp, and, if they tired of that, occupy themselves
in ornamenting our villa, and in improving its sleep-
ing-apartment with a roof—so that, in case we abode
here another night, we might be able to sleep without being drenched with the rain.

In accordance with this arrangement, the Master and the artist, with Powell and Conway, prepared
themselves for the day, and set out on their enterprise of discovery. The heavens seemed to favor us,

for we had scarce yet filed into the stream, when the sun broke through the vapor of the valley and lit up the windings of the little river, until it shone all resplendent of gold, and amber, and snow-white foam. It was as if some celestial light had suddenly illumined the dripping and cheerless Canaan, and we went

> "On our way attended
> By the vision splendid."

Some short distance below the camp, when in the middle of a small, grassy island, we saw a large doe standing about fifty yards below us, among a group of rocks in the middle of the stream, where she was browsing upon the moss. Presently she saw us, and raised her head, standing motionless and lost in wonder—irresolute as Ariadne when she was about to fly.

"She has fawns," whispered Powell, "back in the laurel, and has left them for a while, to come down into the river to drink, and eat the moss upon the rocks."

"Don't stir," whispered Conway. "Keep still as you can, till I go back to the camp and get my rifle. It's an elegant shot!"

The Master clapped his hands, and the deer bounded in about two leaps to the bank of the river, and disappeared—vanished.

"No, Conway," said the Master, "you wouldn't kill that beautiful creature, in cold blood!"

"We hunters," replied the old forester, in some amazement, "don't think about their beauty, Mr. Philips; it's their meat we look at."

"It's as well not to have shot it, Conaway," said Powell. "She has fawns over there in the laurel."

"How do you know that?" asked the Signor.

"Why, come down to the place, and I'll show you."

We moved down to the rocks and halted. "You see," said Powell, "here are the tracks of that deer coming into the water, and here they are going out. That shows, you see, that she went out the same way she came in."

"Yes."

"You observed she turned round to jump out of the river."

"Yes."

"Well, we hunters reason from this, that she must have fawns over here in the laurel, or she would have taken out on the other side—which was natural, as she was standing with her head that way. What made her turn to get out the same way she came in? Something turned her; and as it is about the time now they have their fawns, I say it was to get back to them."

"The reasoning's good," replied the Signor.

"I am satisfied," observed the Master, "and have learned a little more of the lore of the forest than I knew before."

"If it was worth while," said Powell, "I would go into the laurel and get the fawns for you. But if there is anything I don't like, it is laurel."

Of course, we had no idea of encumbering our-selves with the fawns; so we pursued our way down the stream—now up to our knees in the water—now stooping under some great tree that had fallen across the stream—again along the banks, as they presented a better footway—now through the little meadows of luxuriant grass that skirted the shores of the stream—over islands of great rocks—breaking into the laurel to get round some hanging cliffs—some-times stepping on a slippery stone, and going down soused all over in the water—until at length, some two miles below our camp, we came to the second falls. These are twelve feet high—a clear pitch, and in the shape of a horseshoe. The pool below them looked deep and dark, spotted with flakes of white foam and bubbles, and no doubt contained some large-sized trout. We did not stop, however, to test it, but proceeded on our course.

The sun by this time has risen high above the mountains, and was shining down upon the Canaan with all his refulgence. The river was ever turning in its course, and every few moments some new charm of scenery was given to our view. The atmosphere was soft and pleasantly warm, and the breeze gently fanned the trees. The wilderness was rich everywhere with hues of all dyes, and the banks of the river gleamed for miles with the flowers of the rhododen-dron. A scene of more enchantment it would be dif-ficult to imagine. The forest with its hues of all shades of green—the river of delicate amber, filled with flakes

of snow-white foam—and the splendor of the rhododendron everywhere in your eye. Picture all this in
the mind—then remember that you were far beyond
the limits of the world you had known—and say, was
it of heaven, or was it of earth!

Such pure, unalloyed charm of soul as we felt
that morning, it would be worth any hardship to
enjoy. No disturbing thought had any place in the
mind. It seemed that we had entered into a new existence, that was one of some land of vision. As for
the world we had left, it was as unknown to our
thoughts as if we had never heard of it; it was absolutely lapsed from all memory, and nothing but the
beauty and the bliss of the untrodden Canaan entered into our hearts.

As for myself—without pretending to speak at
all for the Master, or the Signor, or the two hunters—I am certain I had no idea of having ever been
born of woman—no idea of having ever known a passion of mortal joy or sorrow: I was some creation of
an undiscovered paradise (hitherto undreamed of
even) altogether, for those few hours of a new soul.
And it seems to me now, when I revert my thoughts
to that morning's exploration of the Blackwater, that
all the divinities of old fable must have had their
dwelling-place out there; that surely Pan and Faunus
dwelt in those wilds; that Diana lived there, and
Latmos, on whose top she nightly kissed the boy
Endymion, was the mountain that bordered the
Blackwater; that Venus—she of the sea—

Anadyomene, sometimes left the sea-foam and re-
posed her charms in the amber flow of the river; that
Diana the huntress, with all her attendant nymphs,
pursued those beautiful deer I saw; that the naiads
dwelt in the streams, and the sylphs lived in the air,
and the dryads and hamadryads in the woods
around; that Egeria had her grotto nowhere else but
in the Canaan—all the beautiful creations of old
poesy, the spirits or gods that now

"No longer live in the faith of reason,"—

all were around me in the unknown wild—

"The intelligible forms of ancient poets,
The fair humanities of old religion,
The power, the beauty, and the majesty,
That had their haunts in dale or piny mountain,
Or forest by slow stream, or pebbly spring,
Or chasms and watery depths."

—Sometimes the fancy has possessed me that I saw
Undine sitting in all her beauty by the foam of the
little Niagara, the most beautiful of all the falls. Sometimes, too, I have seen Bonny Kilmeney—who was

"As pure as pure could be"—

sleeping on the purple and gold-cushioned rocks,
even as the Shepherd Poet has so exquisitely cre-
ated her—her bosom heaped with flowers, and lovely
beings of the spirit world infusing their thoughts of
heaven into her spotless soul—her

> "Joup of the lilly sheen,
> Her bonny snood of the birk sae green,
> And those roses, the fairest that ever were seen."

All these images, and many more innumerable, of the creations of the genius of mankind, are associated in my mind, henceforth and for ever, with the Blackwater; and although I am fully aware that in here giving expression to these fancies, I run some little risk of stamping this historic narrative with the character of fiction, yet the judicious reader will observe that this chronicle was intended in its inception to be an impress of the body and soul of the expedition—the motions and affections of the mind were to be recorded, as well as the motions and affections of the body—therefore he will see that it is all in keeping with the high aim of our undertaking. In accordance, then, with this just view of things, I have no hesitation in writing it down here, that the whole expedition felt themselves in a paradise all the morning; and I will take this occasion to observe in regard to myself especially, that I know something of the joys of this world—have had my reasonable share, and more too, of the joy that comes of passion—but that perfect bliss of the soul—that feeling of entire happiness, which has no taint of our mortal lot in it—which is beatific, such as an angel ever lives in, I never had any distinct idea of—never anything but a glimmering, vague, mystified conjecture of, until I felt the heaven of that morning down the exquisite stream.

The reader no doubt is a little startled at this apparent extravagance, but let him restrain himself. It is all true, every word of it—as near as any felicities of the English language will convey a meaning; and although he may deem the brain of the chronicler of the expedition a little turned (by thunder may be), yet I call confidently upon Mr. Butcut, upon Adolphus, upon the Master of St. Philips, upon Triptolemus Todd, Esq., upon the Signor, and the two hunters, to say if it does not but poorly convey to their minds the feelings they experienced. Why, Mr. Butcut, forgetful of all his sufferings, grows enthusiastic when he thinks of the Blackwater, even at this day; and Trip chuckles from ear to ear, with a joyous *ugh—uh!* if you but point your finger in the direction of the Alleganies!

While we have stopped to dilate a little on the heavenly delights of the Canaan, the exploring expedition did not stop, but wound its way down the bed of the stream; and presently turning a rocky promontory that jutted the mountain side, the Blackwater, some hundred yards ahead, seemed to have disappeared entirely from the face of the earth, leaving nothing visible down the chasm through which it vanished, but the tops of fir-trees and hemlocks—and there stood on the perilous edge of a foaming precipice, on a broad rock high above the flood, the Signor Andante (who had gone a-head), demeaning himself like one who had lost his senses, his arms stretched out wide before him, and at the top of his

voice (which couldn't be heard for the roar and tumult around him), pouring forth certain extravagant
and very excited utterances; all that could be made
out of which, as the rest drew close to his side, was
something or other about

> —"The cataract of Lodore
> Pealing its orisons,"

and other fragments of sublime madness about cataracts and waterfalls, to be found at large in the writ-
ings of the higher bards.

Not stopping at all to benefit by the poetic and
otherwise inspired outpouring of the wild and apparently maddened artist, thus venting himself to
the admiring rocks and mountains and tumbling
waters around, the expedition stepped out upon the
furthest verge and very pinnacle of the foaming
battlements, and gazed upon the sight, so wondrous
and so wild, thus presented to their astonished eyes.

No wonder that the Signor demeaned himself
with so wild a joy: for

> "All of wonderful and wild,
> Had rapture for the artist child;"

and perhaps in all this broad land of ours, whose
wonders are not yet half revealed, no scene more ·
beautifully grand ever broke on the eye of poet or
painter, historian or forester. The Blackwater here
evidently breaks its way sheer down through one of

the ribs of the backbone of the Alleganies. The chasm
through which the river forces itself thus headlong
tumultuous down, is just wide enough to contain
the actual breadth of the stream. On either side, the
mountains rise up, almost a perpendicular ascent,
to the height of some six hundred feet. They are covered down their sides, to the very edge of the river,
with the noblest of firs and hemlocks, and as far as
the eye can see, with the laurel in all its most luxuriant growth—befitting undergrowth to such noble
growth of forest, where every here and there some
more towering and vast Balsam fir, shows his grand
head, like

"Caractacus in act to rally his host."

From the brink of the falls, where we now stand, it
is a clear pitch of some forty feet. Below, the water is
received in a large bowl of some fifteen or twenty feet
in depth, and some sixty or eighty feet across. Beyond this, the stream runs narrow for a short distance, bound in by huge masses of rock—some of them
cubes of twenty feet—then pitches down another fall
of some thirty feet of shelving descent—then on down
among other great rocks, laying about in every variety
of shape and size—all the time falling by leaps of more
or less descent, until it comes to something like its usual
level of running before it begins the pitch down the
mountain. This level of the stream, however, is but

"The torrent's smoothness ere it dash below;"

for it leads you to a second large fall, a clear pitch again of some forty feet. From the top of this you look down some two hundred feet more of such shelving falls and leaping descent, as we have described above, until you come again to another short level of the stream. This, in its turn, is the approach to another large fall. Here the river makes a clear leap again of about some thirty feet, into another deep basin; and looking on below you, you see some two hundred feet or more of like shelving falls and rapid rush-down of the stream, as followed upon the other large falls. Getting down below all these, the river having now tumbled headlong down some six hundred feet, more or less, in somewhere about a mile, it makes a bend in its course, along the base of the mountain to the left, and mingles its amber waters with the darker flow of the Cheat: the Cheat some three times the size of the Blackwater; and roaring down between mountains (twelve or fifteen hundred feet sheer up above us), through, not a valley, but a rocky and savage chasm, scarcely wide enough to hold the river.

It will be perceived from this description, that the falls of the Blackwater must be extremely grand, picturesque, and wild, in their character. A stream of good size, that breaks down through one of the bold Allegany mountains—a fall in the whole, of some six hundred feet, must affect the mind grandly. If, instead of a beautiful little river of some fifty feet in breadth, running some two or three feet deep in the main, it were as large as the Cheat, the predominating sense of the beautiful that now belongs to it, would be lost in the terror it would inspire. As it is, let the floods get out in the mountains—let the snows of winter linger on in the Alleganies into the spring; and all at once let the south wind blow, and the sun returning higher up this way, pour down his rays; then would you behold such a mad rush and tumult of waters, roaring down the Alleganies, as would strike such awe into your soul, as not even Niagara, in all his diffused vastness, could impress you with. But, then, it would be no longer the exquisite Blackwater, filling the mind with so wondrous and wild a sense of beauty, that now makes it a picture, such as no son of genius, who had once hung it up in the galleries of his brain, would ever take down.

But enough of comment. We will leave the falls to the imagination of the reader, who can now work up for himself, from the sketch we have given, such a picture as will best please him; and go on to relate some little incidents of fishing, which we hope will impart some pleasure.

If we remember aright, we left the expedition standing on the brow of the first fall, in some considerable tumult of soul at the grand sight that had broken so suddenly and unexpectedly upon them; and the artist—the Signor Andante, in a frenzy of inspiration—

> "On a rock, whose haughty brow
>   Frowns o'er Blackwater's foaming flood,
>   Robed in the ragged garb he wore,
>   With flashing eyes the artist stood;"

now repeating wildly to the Blackwater flood, the fiery song which the last of the bards uttered over "Old Conway's" (I don't mean Conway the man, but the river).

We are happy, however, in being able to inform all who take any interest in the artist, that he did not conclude his rant in the grand manner of the last of the bards; who—

> "Spoke, and headlong from the mountain's height,
>   Deep in the roaring tide, he plunged to endless night!"

No, Andante backed himself very carefully out from the edge of the torrent; and, very much in accordance with our preconceived estimate of him as a man of sense, followed the hunters into the hanging side of the mountain, where he, like the rest of us, letting himself down by clinging to the branches of laurel, and sliding on his back down the steep rocks, with the aid of an occasional precarious foothold, at length succeeded in getting below the cataract.

We now prepared ourselves for the trout. It was by this time, near the middle of the day, too late, as we supposed, for any very good fishing; for the large fish generally by this time lie about in the bed of the streams, and are indifferent to the lure of the bait.

Notwithstanding this, we had scarcely thrown our lines into the deep water before us, before our bait was seized. The Master drew up the first fish. He had thrown in just at the edge of the foam and spray of the fall, and a quick, bold pull swept his line through the foam. On the instant, with a switch of his rod sidewise, then throwing it up aloft, he *landed*, between his thighs (for it was water all around him) a fine vigorous trout, breaking off about two feet of the switch-end of his maple rod. This trout was a foot long, and some three inches deep behind the shoulders. Presently Powell drew out another of about the same size. Then the artist brought out a fine one from the bowl. And Conway, who by this time had picked up the best stick he could find, and tied a short bit of sea-weed to it—squatting down on his haunches, on a mossy rock, and looking the picture of some old sleepy satyr of the woods, pulled out his large fish without a word to anybody. It was great work; and the excitement intense. In the course of a quarter of an hour we had caught, among all of us, some twenty fine fish—some of them thirteen inches long—and this with no other bait than the common red worm. Indeed, if to take a quantity of trout be your only object, so full is the stream of them, and so ravenous are they, that with any sort of a line, and anything of a hook—a pin-hook if you can get no other—you may take as many as you can carry. But our tackle was good, and with the exception of a regular rod (which it would have been troublesome to have brought along upon so difficult an enterprise) we were reasonably well provided for the sport. If the reader will bear it in mind, that the Blackwater never in all probability had a line thrown in it before, he need wonder at nothing we can tell him about the quantity of trout it contains, or the greediness with which they bite at any sort of bait.

As our purpose to-day was rather to explore the falls than fish, we drew up our lines and proceeded down the torrent. By dint of much scrambling, and crawling, climbing, leaping, hanging, and every other sort of means you can think of, of getting yourself along—sometimes swept down by the strength of the current, and lodged in some side eddy or pool—driving out the trout, and getting up and shaking yourself, with some two or three craw-fish, about the size of your hand, sticking to your clothes—we made our way down below the second of the large falls. Here we fished again for a while, and caught some fifty more trout; some of us baiting our hooks with the gullets of the fish, cut out for that purpose; and some with the red fins, which we would cut off and use, by way of substitute for the fly, and which was found to answer the purpose as well as anything else.

Satisfied with the trial of the stream here, we drew up, and proceeded down our rugged way. Presently, missing the artist, who had gone ahead of us, we were under some apprehension that he had fallen down some of the rocks, and ended his mortal career, here and elsewhere—especially, when, after repeated calls, we could hear no answer from him. Moving down the stream, therefore, somewhat rapidly, we came upon a wide rock, over which the water lay about in pools; and where we saw scattered about, high and dry, a goodly number of large trout, dying and dead. Below this rock the Signor had let himself down some ten feet; and standing on a flat ledge, enveloped in spray from the water flowing down on either side of him, he was intently engaged in hauling out from a pool before him, the fine trout we saw around about as fast as he could bait his hook. He told us he had been here only some fifteen minutes; and when he ascended, without a dry shred upon him, from the watery grotto wherein he had enshrined himself, he gathered up some sixteen fish of the largest size we had taken that day.

Leaving our rods at this point, we went on as rapidly as we could make our way, down the falls, and finished our exploration to the mouth of the Blackwater. Here, sitting down to rest, we summed up our review of the falls—in which we settled down to the estimate above given, that the leap-down of the Blackwater must be some six hundred feet, in somewhere about a mile. The reader will understand that this estimate is made, not by guesswork, but upon some certain data; for we measured all the larger falls. It will be perceived, however, that we can not be far wrong in our computation, when we make the statement, that from the top of each of the larger falls, you see, at the distance of a few hundred yards down before you, the tops of fir-trees (their bodies not visible) peering up like bushes; and when you get down to them, you find they are great trees of some hundred feet or more in height. Standing upon the top of the first large fall, you look down upon some hundred and fifty feet or more, of the leap-down of the river—going down, then, to this point, you make a turn for some distance, and presently come upon the next large fall—from the top of which you look down upon about the same descent—and so on to the third. But enough. Let us now go back.

About half way up the falls a thunder-storm passed over us; and the reverberation down the chasm was exceedingly grand. Stopping under a hanging rock that afforded us shelter from the storm, we saw in the wet sand the footprints of otter, and other evidences of their inhabiting the stream. Presently there came a volleyed discharge of the heaven's cannon; and as the roar muttered itself away throughout the refts of the mountains, the sun broke out, and we proceeded on our way up the steep ascent—a rainbow over-arching the waterfalls, and the spray everywhere golden with sunbeams. At length, reaching the top of the grand chasm, and standing again on the brink of the impending rocks where we first hailed so rapturously, the leap-down of the river—we took a last look of the wild scene and went on our way to the camp.

Somewhere about five o'clock in the evening we came in, and depositing our spoils of the stream—about a hundred and fifty fine trout; we eat and recounted our adventures alternately, until we and our audience grew tired and fell asleep; the Prior murmuring as he went off, the noble lines of Byron—

"The Assyrian came down like a wolf on the fold,
And his cohorts were gleaming in purple and gold,"—

the Assyrian to his imagination being the dark and rushing Cheat, and *the cohorts gleaming in purple and gold,* the golden Blackwater and the other glittering streams of the Canaan.

CHAPTER XIII.

HOW WE GOT OUT OF THE CANAAN—AND IN SPITE OF OUR TEETH.

Morning has dawned again upon the camp, and with it we arose to prepare for our homeward march. We took our last bath in the Blackwater, and at breakfast eat up all that remained of our provisions. Some of us, sated with the trout, breakfasted entirely upon the bacon that was left. In our hardy and rough life, the fish had ceased to be food to us, and a beefsteak would have been the greatest of luxuries. Had we been prepared to remain out longer, it will be seen, therefore, that we would have taken to killing the deer for our table—which we only did not do heretofore, because it seemed like wanton butchery to slay the beautiful "foresters," when we had the finest of all fish that swim in such abundance. Everything, however, was now gone—the ham and middling eaten, the last of the coffee drank—and not a crumb of bread remained. There were about three hundred trout, cleaned and ready for use, in our kitchen, but we turned up our noses at them. Out of these, Conway selected some of the finest, and making a basket of the bark of the fir-tree, packed them up to take home, no one else choosing to be troubled with them: all the rest we left on the rock—a feast for the otters, or whatever other of the wild inhabitants of the Canaan, who were fond of fish.

With our wallets strapped on our shoulders, and all equipped for the march, we waited the rising of the sun, to marshal us the way we should go; for having no compass along, the god of day was our only guide, preserver, and friend. Presently, the sun arose, "blushing discontented" at the clouds around, and Powell, with his rifle in one hand and the frying-pan in the other, started up from his seat, followed first by Conway, then by all of us—and thus we broke our way into the laurel, making straight up the mountain, that rose high above us, dark and dense with all the green leaves of summer.

Reaching the top of the ridge, the hunters held some counsel as to their course; and telling us, confidently, that they would take us to the glade on the Potomac, where we had left our horses, by two o'clock, we strode through the wild in high spirits—even Peter vaunting himself very much, and proclaiming the glorious feelings of a life in the woods. With much jest, and a good deal of extravagant utterance of one sort and another—some occasional practical remark in regard to the wealth of land and water around us—we went careeringly on our way, like a band of Indians single file on a war-path, if path that can be called where path there was none.

In about two hours of such walking, a damper was put on our spirits by the announcement of gathering clouds. Presently down came the rain; and a little tired already with the climbing up and down the mountains, and the rough and tumble of it all—the *tumble* done in the main by Trip, who fell along as was his wont—we stopped at length under a tree, until the shower, as we supposed it, would pass by. We sat here for some time, but the forest being by this time entirely wet—which of course would wet us in walking through it—we concluded that we might as well take the rain in one shape as another, and proceed on our way. But here at once a question arose as to where the way was, for we had lost the sun to guide us. A right sharp debate took place, but Powell insisting upon a certain direction, off we started—Peter beginning to show a little gloom of countenance, and none of us a face of the brightest. However, on we went, forcing a spirit we did not entirely feel, and after about two hours more of hard walking, all wet and very well blown, we came to a halt at an exclamation made by Galen, the purport of which was, that a bent tree just before us, was the very same bent tree that we had stopped under two hours ago. This was a very discomforting remark to have thrust upon us, and was controverted by the whole party. And there was great difficulty in deciding the matter, for the wilderness is so covered everywhere with moss, and so entirely trackless, and there are so many places that look alike, and so many trees bent over by the storms all about, that the fact of our having been here two hours before was about being decided in the negative (the wish being father to the conclusion), when the doctor discovered a cut in the side of a tree, where he had stuck his hatchet when he was here before.

This settled the question. It was clear we had been walking the last two hours in a circle, and had come back to the point we started from. Clouds now gathered over the countenance of the expedition, about as dark as those over the face of the heavens; and each one manifested himself according to his temper under adversities—defied or bemoaned his fate. A great disputation was immediately entered upon, as to where the north was. Even Powell and Conway differed entirely. Peter vehemently urged it was here—Triptolemus contended it was there. The Signor tried to make it out by the dark side of the trees; but, in the gloom of the day, they were on all sides dark. Galen twisted his neck to no purpose, looking up for a light spot in the clouds by which to place the sun. The Prior said and did nothing, but looked as if he had come to the conclusion that the Canaan had no north.

"There is nothing clear about the whole matter," exclaimed Peter, gloomily, "but that we are lost!"

"That's clear as preaching," answered Trip.

"What an infernal idiot I was to get into this scrape!" continued Peter. "A man with a family—living in ease and comfort, enjoying the society of my friends—I may say surrounded by everything a man ought to desire—in fact, more too!—But such is man!—to come out here into this crooked wilderness, where there is nothing straight—no paths—nothing leading anywhere! Lost—yes, undoubtedly lost, and with a fine chance of being either starved or walked to death—both, I dare say!"

"Or eaten by the bears," said Trip.

"Any bear that attempts that game on me," rejoined Peter, "would play into my hand."

"Gentlemen," observed the Signor, "there is nothing gained by staying here, that I can see. I propose that Conway take the lead, as he and Powell differ about the course. Let's try his luck, and see what will come of it."

"Agreed," said Powell; "let Conaway try it: but you are going the wrong way. Here, more to the left, I say, we will come upon the horses. Here's the north, and here's northeast—and northeast is our course."

"What do you judge from, Powell? The skies are all clouds; you can't judge by the moss, and the weather-stains on the trees—for they are on all sides alike."

"Well, I can't say rightly what I judge from. But there is something in the shape of the hills—the way they slope—and the looks of the country, that makes me say here's the northeast; and I believe in an hour or two we would come right down on our horses."

Powell was evidently very much mortified at his having walked us round in a circle for the last two hours. But he accounted for it satisfactorily enough, by reminding us that in sitting down here before, and shifting our position under the trees to avoid the rain, we had unconsciously lost sight of the direction we were on; and starting off in the confusion of a disputation upon the vexed question as to where the sun was, we had, without consideration, taken the direction we happened to be facing at the time. An intelligent man, like Powell, takes great pride in his knowledge of the woods; and in proportion as he estimated his knowledge highly, he was now greatly mortified, as was evident from his whole bearing. The doctor, seeing this, from the kindness of his nature stepped in to the mortified forester's relief.

"Never mind it, Powell," he observed, blandly. "It don't at all impugn your woodcraft in our opinion. Daniel Boone himself would get lost out here in a cloudy day. But let Conway try it for a while, as proposed. It's just trying his luck, you know— which may fail too."

"I would rather Powell should keep the lead—he

knows more about the woods than I do," said old Conway, a little infirm of purpose.

"No, I have missed it once," observed Powell, "and it's but fair that Conway should try it."

"It's no such mighty matter," said Trip; "I could do it myself!"

"I'll bet," answered Peter, "that if we were to follow you, we wouldn't get five miles away from where we are now standing in the next three weeks!"

"Your *luck*, Trip," said the Master, "couldn't bring us out, by possibility, anywhere else than at the exact opposite point to that we are aiming for!"

"Ugh—uh!" replied Trip. "If you follow me, I'll hit the Fairfax stone in an hour. I feel, and have felt, all the morning, somehow, as if it ought to be over here. And you all know, gentlemen, I've a sort of lean that way."

"That's exactly my opinion," said Powell. "I would be willing to bet on it, that it is just in the direction Mr. Todd says. That's the course I've been arguing for with Conaway."

"Come, give up the point, Powell."

"Blast the crooked wilderness, that I should have got turned around so! I a'n't worth anything any longer!"

"Never mind it, Powell. Man is prone to error."

"That's what old Davy Waddell says," observed the doctor.

"How was that, Adolphus?"

"You all know Davy, gentlemen—"

"Yes—a very shrewd, clear-headed man."

"And a very original one."

"The state hasn't a more remarkable one in its limits."

"That's a risky remark—there are so many of them! But what about Davy?"

"Well, I'll tell you," resumed the doctor. "Some years ago, I was at the races down at Baltimore—about the time the Central club was in its hey-day—before racing had died down in the country. Stevens's 'Black Maria' had beaten the Southern horse in the great race of the season. But a race was made by Colonel Johnson, to run 'Trifle' against the Northern mare the next day. Trifle was then young, and pretty much unknown. Trifle beat the race. There was a great deal of excitement about, and a good deal of money lost and won. After the race was over, I walked up to the hotel, where there was a great crowd, and a good deal of loud talking, laughing, and paying over of money, going on. In the midst of all this *melée*, Davy's voice sounded high above it all, and compelled attention. It seems that the most of the betters had staked upon Black Maria—and very naturally too, for she had won the race of the day before against one of Johnson's best horses—the 'Bonnets of Blue,' I believe. Davy, however, had bet on Trifle, and of course he won. He was accordingly in high spirits, and was consoling the losers by explaining to them how prone man was to *arrar*, as he called it:—

"'Gentlemen, I tell you, you needn't think any the worse of yourselves for betting on the wrong mare, for I wish I may never see another horserace if man a'n't always committing arrar in some shape or other. It a'n't in his nature to avoid it! Why, sar, let any man—any intelligent man—any of you gentlemen around me—any man, sar, who doesn't know the geargraphy of the country he's a riding in, come to a place in the woods where the roads fork, and he's sure to take the wrong fork—he's sure to do it, sar! And, gentlemen, if there's a cock-fight a transpiring anywhere, the most of the betters are sure to pick out the fowl that's whipped—I never knew it otherwise! Pitch up a handful of coppers in the middle of a bar-room that's full of people, and some two or three, by chance—altogether by chance—will say, "Heads," but all the rest of them will call out, "Tails!" and when you come to pick up the coppers, it's heads they all are: I never knew it otherwise, unless thar was some cheating going on. And now, gentlemen-losers, I'm going to take the liberty of giving you a little advice—I always practise on it—and I don't know that I ever lost any money except when I've been foolhardy enough to go against it: and that is, always to be against the majority; for I'll be d——d, sar, if I ever have known 'em to be right, except when it was clearly by chance! You see it must be so— for, seeing as how man is prone to *arrar*, the majority of 'em must go wrong; and the majority being necessarily wrong, whenever you want to bet your money upon a race, or cock-fight—at faro, or "sweat," or "double O," or anything at all at which gentlemen pleasure themselves—find out the general opinion, and put up your money against it, as I did on the Virginia mare on principle, and you'll double your pile!—you may depend upon it, as sure as my name's David Waddle, at your service!'"

"Well, now," said old Conway, "that Waddell must be considerable of a smart man; for whenever I've been out in the woods, and didn't know I was right, I've mostly, I may say, gone wrong."

"What's the opinion here, gentlemen," inquired Peter, "in regard to the northeast?"

"That question has neither a majority nor minority attached to it. There are no two of us who agree on it."

"Allow me to say, gentlemen," observed Peter, "that this thing is not to be trifled with. It's a very serious business. Now, it strikes me that there is something in Davy Waddle's opinion, and that we ought to act upon it. Something might come out of it. Let every man, I say, point to where he thinks the north is."

It was done, on the word; and the fact was demonstrated that the expedition entertained seven different opinions on the subject. Of course, it was impossible, in our case, to act on Waddell's theory of going right, and we had to give up that chance. One of three things, therefore, was all that was left to us: either to follow Powell, who had just walked us round for two hours in a circle; or trust to Trip's lean to the Fairfax stone; or stake our deliverance upon old Conway, who seemed by no means confident in his judgment. Something, however, had to be done; and, as is usually the case in such matters, we adopted the wrong alternative—put Conway in the lead, and went to the right, when we should have gone to the left, as it afterward turned out.

Now, then, Conway leading, we once more broke our way through the wild, striking a course that presently brought us to some laurel. This we skirted for a while, but at length found ourselves hemmed in by a great belt of it, spreading everywhere as far as the eye could see. There is always a stream of some size in the laurel; and we now plunged into the brake to see in what direction the water flowed. If it ran to the right hand, both the hunters agreed that we would be on the waters east of the Backbone, flowing into the Potomac—and would be on the right course; if it ran to the left, it would then be certain that we were still west of the Bone, on the waters of the Cheat—and therefore on the wrong course altogether. When we made our way to the stream, it ran to the left; and hope now put off farther than ever. There was evident dismay upon the countenance of the expedition, and something of a disposition manifested to revolt against the guides—which shows that, notwithstanding all the talk about man's individual advancement in this nineteenth century, he is, in and about, the precise same animal at bottom now

that he was when he murmured at the leading of
Moses and Aaron in the Arabian wilderness. However, be this as it may, there was evidently nothing
to be gained by mingling our murmurs, here in the
wilds of the Canaan, with the gentler murmurs of
this unknown little stream. So we crossed over the
laurel—which gave us about as much to do as we
could attend to for the time—and, right or wrong,
kept on the way we were going; and after about an
hour's hard and rather disconsolate work, we came
to a halt, on the top of a ridge, to rest ourselves, and
let Peter come up with us, who by this time was farther behind than was deemed consistent with his
safety. Presently, that unhappy gentleman came in,
looking very much dismantled—his face red—breathing hard—and renewing, for about the hundred and
nineteenth time (according to Triptolemus's arith-
metic), his proposition to encamp.

"Oh, this is most damnable!" exclaimed Peter.
"What o'clock is it?"

"You had better ask, 'What's the latitude?'"

"I take it," said Powell, "it is somewhere between
dinner-time and supper-time."

"Is there anything to eat?" asked Peter. "I'm suffering for food; my strength is nearly gone!"

"Conway, give him a raw trout out of your basket," replied the artist.

"Have you any bread?" inquired Peter.

"Not a crumb."

"Nor any meat?"

"No meat—not a bite!"

"Well, that settles it—we must encamp, and let the hunters go out and shoot a deer."

"No, not so, we must get into the settlements at all hazards," interposed the artist.

"If the sun would only come out, I'll insure it to reach the horses yet to-day," said Powell.

"If I could have had any idea of this," rejoined Peter—"that I should be walked to death in this manner—I don't think—"

"Don't think anything! It's clear that all we have to do is to go on. We may get out somewhere. If we stay here, we may starve."

At this moment, in the midst of all these doubts and fears of ours, and the perplexity and bewilderment of the guides, some one thought he discerned something like a slight lighting up of the clouds. This led to a very excited debate, maintained with great ability on all sides, whether it indicated the position of the sun, or might not be just as well caused by the wind getting up in that quarter. After a good deal said, however, that we will not stop to record here—all of which was strongly characterized by the different mental and moral peculiarities of the various parties to the discussion—it was at length put to the vote and passed, that no man should henceforth say a word upon the question as to where the four points of the compass were, but that the matter should be left to the two hunters, upon whose deliberations, undisturbed by any suggestions of ours, the fate of the expedition should entirely depend. Powell and Conway, therefore, undisturbed by any confusing opinions of ours, presently came to a determination as to their course, and off we struck again through the wilderness.

We will not encumber our narrative with a recital of all that occurred on the march, but merely state, that the route we had fallen on in our bad luck, led us through about as rugged, as savage, and as difficult a wilderness, as a man could well get into; that we climbed hills so steep that we had to pull ourselves up by clinging to anything we could lay hold of, and get down them as best we could—that we were now all the time either crossing mountain-tops, or clambering their sides, or plunging into the laurel that filled the ravines between; that sometimes the dead trees would cover the ground everywhere before us—lying six feet high when we would come to scale them, and often so decomposed that we would sink into them up to the waist. It was through such a wild that we now forced our way; until, at length, somewhere about five o'clock in the evening, jaded and much exhausted for want of food, that part of the expedition that was in the advance called a halt in front of some very extensive laurel just ahead, the look of which made it necessary, in the opinion of the guides, to hold a council of war.

"This time we straggled in at considerable intervals—an indication of our weary plight; and each one, as he came in, instead of sitting down as usual, unstrapped his wallet, and stretched himself out at full length on the moss, wet as it was from the rain of the day. Up to this time no one had entertained the idea, seriously, that we would not be able to get out of the Canaan some time or other during the day. But that hope was now failing us; and although we had nothing to eat, it was seriously deliberated whether we had not better build a fire and prepare to pass the night where we were. But at this time, the clouds that had obscured the sky all day, broke away, and the wind rising, the sun presently shone out; whereupon it was determined to make one more effort to get out, and if that failed, then to encamp, roast the few trout we had for a supper, and take the chances of killing a deer in the morning for our breakfast.

This determination met with no favor from Peter, who was dead opposed to any further walking for the day. He urged the advantage of encamping in a great many points of view—but all to no avail; and, finally, as a last resort, made an appeal to feeling.

"Well, then, gentlemen, go on. One thing is certain, that I can go no further. You will have to leave me behind, if you can reconcile it to your consciences."

"Man in a state of nature has very little of that commodity," said the Prior.

"As for myself," said the Signor, "I am somewhat at best, like the Spanish sharper, who threw *his* aside in his youth, because he was told it had a *sting*."

"You may make yourselves as merry as you please with my sufferings," replied Peter, with an air of resignation, "but it's utterly impossible for me to go any further. And what is it all for? We are wandering about here, nobody knows where. Gentlemen, it's the height of nonsense. Let's encamp and eat something."

"Hadn't we, Peter, much better keep on a little longer—we might, by chance, get to the horses."

"If we stay here we will never get out," said the Signor. "Powell, move on."

"Stop awhile," said Peter, "let me ask a question of Powell. Powell, have you any distinct idea at all of where we are?"

"Well, to tell you the truth, Mr. Botecote, I have not. All the water we have come upon yet, has been running the wrong way to me. If I could see some water running to the right of our course, I should feel satisfied."

"You really give it up then, Powell?"

"No, I don't say I give it up—I only say I don't know where we are."

"What do you say, Conway?"

"I'd give something to be back on the Blackwater where we started from."

"There it is—I knew it would be so from the beginning. We don't know where we are. These hunters haven't the slightest idea themselves. It's all abominable! It is perfectly intolerable! It's insufferable! It's"—

"It's bad enough, that's true," said one.

"And likely to be worse," said another.

"My heels are rubbed raw," said Galen, "and will be, I expect, rawer before we get out."

"Towells was right about the Canaan," said Trip.

"Towers," said the Signor; "Towers, Trip, don't call him Towells. You only add to Peter's aggravations."

"He's beyond such niceties now," said the Master. "It is only when the body's at ease that the mind is delicate."

"May Towers roast for this!" said Peter. "It's as much owing to him, as anybody else, that I came out into this desert. He took very good care, however, not to come himself!"

The expedition, by this time, was well under way again, skirting the edge of the laurel that lay wide to the left of us, while the mountain, on whose slopes we walked, rose high and bold above us, on the right. Pursuing a course along the rugged and broken side of the mountain, it was not long before we found ourselves entangled in the midst of some fallen trees that blocked up the way. This broke up the single file line of our march; and each man hunted out for himself the best way to get through, in doing which, we became a good deal scattered about the forest. In this dispersion of our forces, it so fell out, that Galen, stopping astraddle of the last monstrous hemlock he had to climb over—his sore heel impelling him thereto—saw something that he took for an old blaze, on a tree before him.

This he announced in a loud voice; and there was a general gathering in of the expedition around him. It was an undoubted blaze. But whether it led to the Potomac settlements, or those in the opposite direction on the Cheat, was all matter of doubt. At all events, it would lead us out somewhere, if it could be traced. With the purpose of forming some opinion in regard to it, Powell followed it for some distance up the mountain—then returned, and traced it down the mountain, until he came to the laurel. Here he called us to him; when he and Conway held a very earnest and excited consultation—the result of which was a declaration, that if the blazing continued on through the laurel, it would, in all likelihood lead us to the Potomac.

Stimulated by the probability of being near the Potomac, we now broke into the laurel, and forced our way through its tangled branches with an impetuosity that made nothing of its difficulties—eagerly hunting out the cuts on the trees—now losing them—now finding them again; until, at length, we came upon something like an old cattle path. Down this we made our way, without any heed to the blaze—half in a run—Triptolemus thrown out into the bushes occasionally—and Peter full up with the movement, even when it was at its fastest. Old Conway was ahead, springing along with the light and nimble movement of a kitten, notwithstanding the rifle on his shoulder, and the basket of fish, the coffee-pot, and tin-cups dangling to his girdle; and presently, he reached the base of the mountain—where he soon came to the banks of a stream, and cried out that it was the Potomac. Powell came up and made proclamation to the same effect; and *The Potomac* was shouted all along our line, as we descended the steeps of what we now knew was the Backbone: the echoes crying out every-where *The Potomac*—the woods and the floods still reverberate with the voices, even as we stood silent on the banks of the laurel-crowned river.

"I knew it, gentlemen, I knew it would be thus. We were bound to get out," said Peter, very extravagant in his happiness—his genuine characteristics beginning to reveal themselves for the first time since we abandoned our horses and took to it afoot. "Yes, gentlemen," he continued, oratorically, "we are out at last—and I will say it, owing to a degree of indomitable energy, perseverance, skill, fortitude, and endurance, and so forth, et cetera, that has never been matched. It is not to be denied, that history contains many instances of desperate achievement, bearing some resemblance to this deliverance of ours—there is the well-known case of Moses in the bullrushes—but what are bullrushes, I would like to know, to this all-fired laurel? Grass! nothing but grass! Napoleon got out from the forests of Russia—but how? With all his grand army gone! We stand here, gentlemen, with our ranks yet unthinned by loss of a single follower. It is true, gentlemen, I was a little disconsolate at one time; but then I recalled to mind the case of Marius sitting among the ruins of Carthage, in the very *acme* of his adversity; and remembering that he was a second time proconsul, my soul rose up within me, and I would have suffered the last extremity of martyrdom in the shape of locomotion, before I would have given up. The case, also, of Moses and the children of Israel occurred to me; and I determined it should not be said by posterity that the children could get into their Canaan, while I wasn't able to get out of ours. I will even, gentlemen, go so far as to say, that at that crisis, when I thought we had found out the perpetual motion, from the rounds we were describing in the forest—I will candidly admit it, out of my regard for the truth of history—that just then, I verily believe I would have submitted to the operation of being eaten by a bear, without feeling any indignation at the audacious effrontery of such a procedure. But Allah Akbar!—God is Great!—and the bounties of Providence are new every day!—and here I am—you may say in spite of my teeth—and, indeed, you may say of all the other parts of my body. When I look back upon my tracks, and think of the laurel, and the interminable mountains—and such mountains, and the piles of rotten hemlocks and firs that I have been stuck in—and that I have been at it now from sunrise, without any intermission, up to this time, six o'clock in the evening—thirteen mortal hours—and all without anything to eat, may the devil take my lights! as Towers says, if I am not utterly lost in astonishment at those powers, hitherto unrevealed to me, that have stood me out. It's glory enough for any one man's lifetime: and I tell you all now, if ever you catch me in the Canaan again, unless it is a horseback, and with plenty of provisions, my name's not Peter Botecote. By the way, men, how far off are the horses from here? That's a matter to be seen to at once."

"Well, I reckon, the glade where we left them, must be some six miles above us," said old Conway.

"At least that," said Powell.

Peter fell again at this information. But upon Conway's saying that it was not more than some three miles to his house through the woods, and by a path all the way, it was determined to let the horses stay where they were, and go on at once afoot.

So we moved on, crossed the Potomac, and struck into a good path winding through the forest. We went along at a rapid walk; and even at this fast gait were urged to go faster by Peter, now dashing along with a free swing up among the foremost of the party. Indeed, you would suppose from the energy of his movements, that he was walking for a wager—so reanimated was he at having accomplished the exodus of the Canaan.

At this rate we walked about an hour—and had yet some two or three miles to go. It was evident that Conway was tolling us along. But on we went, getting down from a pace that was four miles an hour, to one that was only two; and at length crossing

Laurel run (one of the tributaries of the Potomac) we ascended the long hill beyond, at scarcely the rate of a mile an hour.

The lighter part of the expedition rose this hill at evident advantage, and sat down on a log to rest. But weight was now beginning to tell effectually; and the heavy forces advanced at a very slow and labored pace, each one wheeling in upon the log as he came up, except Butcut, who passed on without stopping, or casting even so much as a look to where we sat.

"Don't you mean to stop and blow, But?"

"Blow the devil! I'm blowing all I can as it is!"

"You had better stop—we have two miles yet to go."

And upon this announcement Peter wheeled to, and came down heavily upon a stump near him, without saying a word.

It was evident now that the expedition was very nearly on it last legs. Nothing but that fortitude of endurance, indomitable energy, &c., which Mr. Botecote had alluded to down on the banks of the Potomac, had kept it moving up to this time. One was a little faint—another was dizzy about the brain—a third had a film over his eyes—Trip said that there was a humming, and buzzing, and singing going on in his ears, very much like the running down of his watch when the main-spring breaks: every one had something out of gear—even Powell and Conway were overtasked; and it is certain that nothing but "the unconquerable free-will" of some of us, and "the undying hope" of all, to get into

Conway's, kept us from remaining out all night starved in the woods, unless, maybe, it was a small flask of brandy, containing about a gill, which the Prior, with a wise forethought, had brought along with him as physic for his body in case he should be bit by a rattlesnake.

The flask was now produced, and each man swallowed a mouthful of it raw. Thus temporarily propped up, we once more set forward on the march; and straggling wearily along the now broad and beaten path, with long intervals between—almost utterly exhausted, we at length, late in the twilight, defiled from the woods into the open fields of the Conway possession (held by squatter tenure), about as dilapidated a set of adventurers as ever wandered a forest—ragged, tattered, and torn, and all forlorn—starved, haggard, barely able to drag ourselves up the gentle slope that led to the cabin-door—the very contrast of the bright, buoyant, elate, trimly-arrayed, and may we not say it, rather stylish-looking band, that only four days ago had witched the world of these regions with our noble footmanship.

I—the writer of this chronicle—with every faculty of my nature, as I supposed, obliterated by fatigue and starvation—with my head bent down to my breast—entered the threshold of the old forester's door, and, putting out my hand, took hold of what I supposed was the hand (extended to me in welcome) of the mistress of the household; but it was not hers—it was the soft hand, freshly washed, of the old man's lithe daughter of seventeen summers; and I take it upon me to say that, broken down as I was, the touch thrilled every fibre of my heart—and I raised my head and looked into the face of the seventeen summers before me—beheld the red of her check and the beam of her young eye—and for the moment I thought she might be Donna Maria Gloriana of Spain, or the queen of Sheba in all her glory!—such and so great is the power of "woman divine" over a man who has been associating for some time with nothing but men and bears in a wilderness. Holding Gloriana Conway's hand as daintily as if it had been the queen of Spain's, my soul revived within me. But when I let it go, I relapsed straightway into my former nothingness. It was but like the swallow of brandy, a temporary stimulant, and nothing more; so I acted upon

a sounder philosophy, and dipped in with the rest into the insides of a monstrous pumpkin-pie, that was already more than half-devoured.

"I thank Heaven," said Peter, scarcely intelligible, owing to an over-large mouthful, "for this deliverance!" And as his heart revived within him, he grew classical, and repeated with much unction the happy words which Gil Blas wrote over his door at Lirias:—

> "Inveni portum. Spes et fortuna valete,
> Sat me lusistis, nunc ludite alios."

"Gentlemen," said the artist, speaking too out of the fullness of his mouth as well as of his heart— "the knight of the gloomy countenance brightens. He has scarcely yet set his foot within the precincts of civilization, and the immortal creation of Le Sage rises unbidden to his thoughts!"

"It is clear But was never intended for savage life," observed one.

"He hasn't made a joke since we've been out," said Trip. "The first time he gave any symptoms of being himself again, was when he made that speech— back on the banks of the Potomac—about Marius and Moses."

"He's lucky he wasn't born an Indian," rejoined the artist.

And to these, and many other such remarks, Mr. Peter Botecote made once in a while a reply; but what he said must for ever remain lost to the world—

for his mouth was so full, that nobody could possibly make it out.

After a satisfactory supper, which in due course of time was prepared for us by the family of the hospitable old hunter—consisting of fried bacon and eggs, broiled venison, some of the trout Conway had brought home, a large coffee-pot of strong coffee, bread, milk, butter, honey, maple-sirup, and various comfits and preserves—which we mention here to show how well stocked is the home of a deer-hunter in the Alleganies—we stretched ourselves out side by side, on some pallets spread down on the floor before the fire, and in a few moments were all dead asleep.

And so ended the day we got out of the Canaan.

CHAPTER XIV.

THE RETURN TO WINSTON—"BOOTLESS HOME AND WEATHER-BEATEN BACK."

WE remained at Conway's next day until about one or two o'clock. Our horses had broken out of the dale on the Potomac, and had returned to Towers's the day after we abandoned them. They had been put back, and again had left—which escapes, in justice to the rhododendron fencing, we must record it, were effected through the barricade at the point of entrance into the dale; in other words, they had escaped by the way they got in: we had not secured the bars effectually. They had been seen passing by Conway's only a few hours before we arrived. Supposing Towers would send them back this morning, we waited, keeping a lookout from the house.

In the meantime, Conway's two boys were despatched to the dale, six miles off, for our saddles and bridles, &c.; and with instructions to go up the mountain beyond, to the Elk-lick, and get Mr. Botecote's Yankee blanket—which was left there hung upon a tree, as the reader will remember, when Peter made his first proposition to turn back.

It was a beautiful morning of the early summer, and we lay idly about on the grass, basking in the sunshine, and commenting upon many things pleasantly enough. As the conversation referred chiefly to our expedition and its incidents, we will relate some of it before we leave.

Mr. Botecote was restored to all his natural vivacity and pleasantry. His eye twinkled, and his countenance was bright. He was again in his proper element of civilization.

"Well, gentlemen," he observed, "I've been thinking about it, and it is my opinion that there is no life like this of the wilderness, after all. It's astonishing, Galen, what an amount of hardship a man can endure! No man can tell what he is until he is tried. Powell, do you think that tract of land can be bought?"

"No doubt of it, Mr. Botecote."

"How many acres are there?"

"Five thousand."

"And for how much?"

"Sixty cents an acre."

"That's three thousand dollars. I'll buy it."

"It's the finest tract in all the country; there's not fifty acres of bad land in the whole of it, and it's all finely watered," answered Powell, encouraging the purchase.

"I'll join you in the purchase, Peter," said Adolphus. "As soon as we get back to Winston, we'll write, right away, and secure it."

"I'm afraid we've lost Peter and Adolphus," observed the artist.

"Oh, that's certain—indeed, I doubt whether they will go back with us at all," replied the Master.

"I can't imagine a more happy life," said Peter, "than a man could live out here—here in the midst of these grand mountains, these noble trees, these perfect waters; the wilderness close at hand for his recreation, with its innumerable deer and trout; the railroad only some ten or twenty miles off, and which you can reach by a road through beautiful glades all the way—that is, after you have got over the Backbone. Adolphus, we must build ourselves a lodge upon our estate. I shall construct something after the old Saxon architecture, that shall look baronial—have great, huge fireplaces, to burn whole loads of wood in at a time;—and a big hall, hung round with trophies of the chase——"

And here Galen broke in: "Yes—and when our friends come up, we will summon Powell and Conway, and all the other foresters, and make inroads into the wilderness—encamp out there, and fish, and shoot the deer."

"Deer!—Nothing so small as that—bears and panthers—elk at the least," said the artist.

"I would have the Canaan as a park," said the Master, "and cut, But, drives through the gorges and defiles of the mountains; bridge the laurel, and have a tower at the falls of the Blackwater, with a good cook in it—such a one as Peter would recommend—

and lounges and cushions of the softest—with a harp or so, and two or three grand pianos, to play swelling themes in accord with the sublime music of the torrent roaring down the Alleganies!"

"I am not building castles, gentlemen," observed Peter with earnestness; "far from it, gentlemen! Never was more in earnest in my life. Why, that five thousand acres, and the others that I would buy in the course of time, would be an immense inheritance to my children! Why, sir, in twenty years, the whole of it would be worth fifty dollars an acre at the least. The railroad, when finished, will open out the country to market at once: it will make tidewater at your door! As fine a country as our Valley is, I would infinitely rather live here!"

Mr. Peter Botecote, it will be perceived, was a very altered man in his feelings this morning. He was no longer the knight of the gloomy countenance. But rowdy and ragamuffin as he seemed externally to the eye, the soul of Philip Sydney was in him, or any highly imaginative, poetic, and sublimated gentleman; and Hope spread before him all her illusions—

"Smiled, enchanted, and waved her golden hair"—

and all-happy visions of the wilderness didn't spare his aching sight. But, we are not deriding Peter. Much of that gentleman's enthusiasm has substantial foundation. The railroad must put this noble country alongside of the sea; and the forest must be cleared away for the plough, and the water-power everywhere must be used, and the coal dug out of the earth, and the ores, the gypsum, the salt, and the lumber, turned into wealth; and therefore the land (such land! that can be bought now from sixty cents to a dollar an acre!) must be worth fifty dollars—and that at no very distant day. But all this is to be done by the hardy enterprise of men in whose souls poetry and imagination are not predominant—by men with necessity at their elbow, who are resolute upon acquisition, and who have been trained to the rougher realities of life; not by a set of daintily-nurtured gentlemen, to whom life has been but little else than an agreeable pastime, whose disquiet has been only the loss of some pleasurable gratification, whose greatest suffering has consisted in being lost for a day in the wilds of the Canaan—a wilderness—but a wilderness of plenty of deer and trout.

"Peter is delightful to me this morning, gentlemen; I never saw a happier countenance," observed the Master.

"Perfectly delicious," responded the artist; "he's blossoming like the rose in the wilderness:—

> " 'O my love is like the red, red rose,
>   That's newly blown in June!' "

"He is happy, sure enough," said Trip. "And he looks natural to me to-day out of his eyes. But yesterday, sitting down on that soft, mushy log, I don't think his nearest neighbor would have recognised him."

"There was a grand gloom on him just about that time: he looked like the pictures of Napoleon on the rock at St. Helena."

"I never had any idea of Philips *grand, gloomy, and peculiar—a sceptred hermit,* &c., before. I see now, however, distinctly the sort of picture of a man the Irish orator must have had in his mind."

"Signor, you ought to have sketched him."

"I have him in my mind's eye, gentlemen: Marius, sitting among the ruins of Carthage, won't be able to hold a candle to him, after I shall have limned him!"

"Trip, you needn't say anything," retorted Peter; "for when the hunters admitted we were lost, your eyes grew very big."

"Well, it did look a little scary to me about that time," answered Trip, "particularly when I saw the Signor there hunting about for the snails, and putting them in his pockets. You see, I thought of Towell's story about the lost man out there. And, now I think of it, I shall retract to Connells my disbelief as soon as I get a sight of him."

"Call him *Towers,* if you please, my dear fellow, Trip; just put your mind upon it—*Towers—Towers!* It would be some amends to him."

And here Peter frankly acknowledged the fact that he was very much broken down and a good deal disconsolate at times; but that, notwithstanding, the pleasure of the expedition was very great to him.

"And, gentlemen," he continued, with much enthusiasm, "I'll go in with you again, at any time you may choose to name, provided only you let me have about a month's notice, so that I may put myself in training beforehand. Indeed, I think, the next time, I'll take it afoot from home. They have got to making these wagons now to run so easy, that a man who uses them must lose eventually all his walking powers—that fine elasticity of muscle—that wiry agility—that free, unimpeded respiration—that everything that is native and to the manner born, I may say, to man, as my experience of the wilderness satisfies me—that—in fine, gentlemen, I shall foot it, I think, for the rest of my days!"

"Right, Peter—down with the wagon!" said the artist.

"And up with the saddle-horse again!" replied the Master. "I will join with you in any reformation of the times that has for its object the ascendancy of the saddle. Bring the republic back to that, and I shall have hopes of it. This foot-work is sufficiently cared for over the land; any fellow that has two legs can get at it. But how many of our people are there of this generation who can ride a real horse! Cavalry are as essential to our national greatness as infantry. While many go afoot, it is essential that some at least should go a-horseback. Where would the nation be to-day, if it had not been for that race of men who were trained in the saddle—those men of 'earth's first blood'—the *gentlemen* who rode the blooded horses that were descended from the loins of the Godolphin Arabian? Don't tell me, Peter, that these men, heroic as they would have been anyhow, had not some elevation given to their heroism by the nobilities of nature begotten of the saddle. Imagine Washington without his charger! Think of him, if you can, afoot! Or can the idea of him even enter into your brain, as a man driving a fast trotter, at about two twenty, over a plank-road! *Could* Alexander of Macedon ever have been Alexander the Great, had he not been *the* Alexander who *could* ride Bucephalus? Shakspeare understood all about it when he made Richard rage about Bosworth-field for a *horse!*"—

"'A horse! a horse! my kingdom for a horse!'"—

here ranted Peter, breaking in upon the Master; and, throwing himself into a very theatrical position, he went on, and enacted the whole of the battle-scene—out-raging Kean or Booth even—to the great wonderment of Powell and Conway, and the whole of Conway's family, who came out bewildered to the performance. At length, having got through the play, Peter went on to learn from his two foresters the expense of clearing the timber from his proposed estate;—which information was, when summed up and digested, in and about as follows:

A good day-laboror would belt an acre a day; and he could be hired for fifty cents a day. One man, therefore, in a hundred days, would belt or deaden one hundred acres. Ten men, in that time, would belt a thousand acres, and at a cost of five hundred dollars. A thousand acres of the forest then, could be easily deadened by the next spring. As soon as this is done, the ground being freed from the tax made upon it by the growth of the trees, and the sun let in, it would, in the first season, grow up in timothy, the spontaneous growth of these wilds. This thousand acres in that condition would graze, the first year, some five hundred head of cattle, which could be had at a dollar a head for the season. The estate would yield, then, for the first year, five hundred dollars. The next year, the same thousand acres would graze a thousand head of cattle—that is a thousand dollars it would yield the second year. The third year you could harrow over the ground, sow some grass-seed additional, maybe, in places, and go to making hay for winter use. This year you could buy young cattle at eight and ten dollars a piece, and having the hay to keep them over winter, sell them the next year at eighteen or twenty dollars a head. Some two hundred acres of the thousand being kept for hay, you could cut from them at least two tons to the acre. A ton of hay is good allowance for the support of a steer through the winter. Therefore you could keep some four hundred head over the winter; four hundred would be worth seven or eight thousand dollars gross—equal to some three or four thousand dollars clear. The fourth year the roots of the trees would be all dead, and your land fit for cultivation—for raising wheat, rye, oats, potatoes, or whatever else the climate and soil would allow; and by this time the land kept in timothy would grow from three to five tons of hay to the acre.

From this digest of the information communicated by Powell, the reader will perceive that the speculation will be a grand one in a money point of view; and Peter and Adolphus were already, in their mind's eye, great cattle-raisers, with numerous herdsmen, and almost innumerable bullocks over their vast possessions—say some fifty thousand acres apiece—here on the slopes and lawns of the Backbone; and their houses were filled, during the summer months, with gentlemen and ladies, who hunted and rode, fished, eat the trout, the broils, and roasts and pastries of the deer, with bear's meat, and panther or wild-cat collops—grew fat and defied the world below, in the pastimes of the wilderness—then a wilderness made easy of ingress and egress by fine graded roads, cut out by the great proprietors, Peter and Galen—whose two castles of old Saxon architecture, built on either slope of the mountain, would enable the Backbone to frown down on the Potomac on the one side, on the Blackwater on the other, as—

> "The castled crag of Drakenfels
> Frown's o'er the wide and winding Rhine."

In the meantime, while all this future was entering deep into the hearts of the two lords paramount of these regions—the duke of Canaan, and the baron of the Backbone—Andante and the Master were stretched out upon the grass, a little distance off, commenting upon the scene around them.

"Did you ever see a more perfectly ruffian-looking couple of fellows in your life, than those two great landholders yonder."

"They put me in mind of the vagabond banditti that used to infest the stage in Fra Diavolo."

"I don't think you look any better, Guy!"

"Nor I, you Signor! If I were to meet you alone on the highway, I would give you a very wide berth. I don't think I have ever seen in painting, or read of in description, a more unmitigated ruffian than you look!"

"Trip, sprawled out yonder, comes up to my idea of a red republican crippled in the leg at a barricade."

"I can understand very well, why we should look like a set of vagabonds who would steal sheep, and pigs, and poultry; but that is not it. There is a look about us of a set of men who would rob, and murder, burn, plunder and ravage a whole country. There is no such look about Powell and Conway."

"I understand it this way," said Andante, "I think it quite likely, that degrade us from our rank as gentlemen—take away all the restraints of civilization from us—in other words, put us down on the Spanish main, and we would discover some qualities that would be considered right respectable among pirates."

"What! do you think that of But!"

"No, I except him. If he was to embark in life on the Spanish main, I think he would be taken and hung."

Here Mr. Butcut, hearing something about his being captured and hung, the visioned bliss, and power, and dominion over great estates, &c., &c., which filled and thrilled his brain all the morning, were all obliterated from his mind by the unhappy idea; and turning his thoughts altogether away from the Blackwater, he entered into a very earnest maintenance of the opinion, that he would make as good a pirate as any gentleman present.

"In fact, gentlemen," he said, concluding his defence of himself, "I believe, barring, always, the walking and starving, I would be as efficient a man as any of you, upon any marauding expedition, whether by sea or land."

"Feed him enough, and carry him—and I believe so too," said Trip.

After this very just remark of Triptolemus's, which was assented to on all hands, our horses came in sight, emerging from the woods; and we began preparations for our departure.

Having paid all expenses at the Hotel Conway, handsomely—shaken hands kindly with all the family (amounting to some eight or ten, big and little), especially taking care not to forget the oldest daughter of the old forester, who had a soft hand and a kindling eye, and was a very modest, and very pretty maiden of some seventeen summers, we turned our steps Towers-ward; and half of us a-foot, and half a-horse, we defiled into the forest, presenting to the eye a very good picture of the vagabond picturesque in scenery. As we went out we might have passed well enough for the nobler order of outlaws—such as Robin Hood, and Little John, and Will Scarlet; and Butcut would have done for the jolly friar—but now, all tattered and torn, the glory of our trim array all gone—our plumage drooping, and general aspect beggarly, we more resembled a band of the inferior banditti who infest the neighborhood of pig-pens and poultry yards. Still we were picturesque of aspect; and as we followed the winding horsepath, up the hill-sides and down the steeps—now through the little streams that made their way to the Potomac—into the dells, and through them, and up out of them again, until we reached the cone of the Backbone; and so, on and along it, until we came out into the northwestern highway—there were many points of view in which an artist could have made a picture of our march, worthy of being hung up anywhere in the halls and bowers of our land. Indeed, the Signor says, that he has it now in his mind's eye, and that some day, when his genius is sufficiently inspired, he will render the expedition as memorable as that of Xenophon, by putting it on canvass as it wound its way out dismantled through the romantic scenery of the Backbone; choosing this one of its many aspects, by which to perpetuate its remembrance, because, as there is dignity in sufferings endured, its great toils and hardships will be impressed more fully upon the mind, by the tatterdemallion aspect that so thoroughly belonged to it, as it approached its end.

After reaching the highway we have nothing more to record, except that the travellers along the road, in every instance, gave us the track by shying off to the right or the left, out of our way; and that they returned our salutation with a glad and subservient courtesy; which shows that the people who travel these regions, are either very civil in their manners, or that they took us for a band of most desperate ruffians, which, we leave the judicious reader to determine. Thus, in full and undisputed possession of the right of way to the whole or any part of the northwestern turnpike that we chose to take, we at length, at about five o'clock in the afternoon of the fifth day, dismounted at Towers's gate, all alive and well—restored by Heaven to the regions of civilization—toughened, roughened, high in health, strong in limb, and joyously elate with the achievement of our hardy enterprise; as—

"Full of spirit as the month of May."

Though not quite so—

"Gorgeous as the sun at midsummer."

And so ends the adventure into the Canaan wilderness of Randolph.

Here, also, ends this Blackwater Chronicle.